Song of Eve

When they had made camp and eaten, all gathered about the fire, and Nathan took out his harp. The men leaned against trees or sprawled upon the ground in relaxed anticipation. His fingers drew from the strings a sweet, plaintive tune familiar to Shaina from her childhood. It was a song of his homeland, and he played it here, tonight, as he rested upon the very borders of that beloved valley. There was a haunting quality to the music, intensified by firelight, sparks drifting upward in the leafy darkness. He had told her once that there were words to the song, words that told of Adam's sorrow upon his dismissal from Eden, and tonight she felt the sadness in her very bones.

Song of Eve

An Allegory of Last Days

June Strong

REVIEW AND HERALD PUBLISHING ASSOCIATION

Washington, DC 20039-0555
Hagerstown, MD 21740

This book was
Edited by Gerald Wheeler .
Designed by Richard Steadham
Cover art by Victoria Poyser
Type set 10/11 Cheltenham Light

PRINTED IN U.S.A.

Unless otherwise noted, Bible texts are from the *Holy Bible, New International Version.* Copyright © 1973, 1978, International Bible Society. Used by permission of Zondervan Bible Publishers.

R&H Cataloging Service

Strong, June (Kimball)
The song of Eve.

I. Title.
220.950 5

ISBN 0-8280-0388-2

CONTENTS

This book is dedicated, with immeasureable love, to my children—Melody, Lori, Kim, Jeff, Mitch, and Amy.

No book is ever written alone. There are those who sustain, those who endure, those who inspire, and those who intercede.

Thank yous
to Don, who shared me with a typewriter for months.

to my grandchildren, who waited patiently for me to come out of seclusion.

to Alta, Howard, Isabel, and others, who prayed without ceasing.

to Shirley, who lovingly volunteered to feed it all into a word processor.

to God, who did not leave me to struggle alone, but walked beside me through an agelong past.

"No one knows about that day or hour, not even the angels in heaven, nor the Son, but only the Father. As it was in the days of Noah, so it will be at the coming of the Son of Man. For in the days before the flood, people were eating and drinking, marrying and giving in marriage, up to the day Noah entered the ark; and they knew nothing about what would happen until the flood came and took them all away. That is how it will be at the coming of the Son of Man" (Matthew 24: 36-39).

THE GIFT

Late-afternoon sunlight played across ivory walls and the deep green tropical plants sprawling against them. Water, whispering over rocks in one corner, made the large, airy room seem almost an extension of the leafy world beyond the open window. A bird, blue as a piece of fallen sky, flitted about a young girl sitting, knees drawn up, on a lounge of softest carded wool. Absent-mindedly she held out her hand to the bird, but one had only to note the dreamy sea-green eyes to know that her thoughts were far away.

"Well, little Sapphire," she said finally, stroking his sleek feathers affectionately, "you have disturbed my reverie, so now you must listen. Father has promised me a surprise tonight, and no ordinary surprise at that. Something very special. And Mother is upset about it. I can tell by the way she walks." The girl smiled, seeing her mother's erect, disapproving carriage once again in her mind's eye. But she has not said no. "Very mysterious, wouldn't you say, my little friend?"

The bird cocked his small head as if he were indeed pondering her question.

"I don't think he's going to buy me something, for he knows I don't yearn after anything in the marketplace. All those silver bangles in which Mother so delights only get in my way when I'm running through the woods or working in the gardens. Perhaps he's going to *make* me something. That must be it." She snuggled the bird under her chin, letting her thick brown hair with its copper highlights fall like a nest about him. "Maybe a sculpted bird as beautiful as you. But Mother would not object to that. Very mysterious, indeed."

Putting the bird back in a large aviary, which filled one corner of the room with color and song, she strolled out through an expanse of flowers, shrubs and green grass toward a long, low structure at the rear of the property. The sight as she entered was a familiar one, but she never tired of it. Her father's workshop was a place of peace despite the constant presence of a workman or two busily tending the firing ovens or preparing the clay. Knowing her father was no ordinary potter, she walked among the tools of the potter's trade. Everywhere there was *blue.* Rejected lumps of blue clay upon the floor, tall blue vases in various stages of production, blue urns, and lovely bowls. But she loved the sculptures best, and she always studied the collection slowly and appreciatively, missing the absent one that had been sold, seeking the new one fresh from her father's hands. Today she spotted a peacock with his tail fanned into subtle shadings of the blue clay. How long had her father labored over that detail? There was a proud turn to the head, so like the peacock that strutted about among the tamarisks in their own rookery. How did he catch these nuances of stance or expression?

Still smiling with pleasure, she turned to where her father molded a deep bowl with sure strokes. She had learned as a child that she was free to come and go in this place if she refrained from speaking while he was at work. So ingrained was the habit that now, at 15, she made no sound as she watched his artistry. When the bowl was complete, he tilted the edges outward and with deft movements formed, from small remains of moist clay, a garland of leaves and flowers to adorn the rim. The girl made a soft sound of delight. Nathan lifted his head, startled at her presence, so absorbed had he been in his work. "So you like it?" he asked. "So do I. Now, my pretty one, let us leave all this river mud behind and find your mother." He stood and stretched wearily, a trim man of startling height with sandy hair and dark, gentle eyes.

He's all earth tones, Shaina thought, scrutinizing him fondly. *His coarse robe, his skin, his eyes, his hair. He's worked with the earth so long, he's become a part of it.* Only Nathan's *working* earth was blue, the lovely gray blues of Havilah river land in the hidden valley of his childhood. It was from those muted clays that he created the rare pieces that brought such extravagant sums at the marketplace. Other men's dun creations might serve for water jugs and cooking pots, but Nathan, son of Sepp, combined his creative genius with a unique medium to produce an artistry rare among men. It had provided his family a place among the wealthy, and as Nathan and Shaina strolled through the gardens surrounding their home, he was grateful, and as ever, a bit surprised that a work he loved had proved so lucrative.

"How did you spend your day?" he asked, turning toward the girl at his side.

"I worked with Ira in my garden till midday," she replied. "We weeded for hours in the hot sun, and it was most uncomfortable, but the results are gloriously worth it. You will see how beautifully the delphiniums set off the white roses, and the new shrubs brought from the mountains are absolutely right on the rocks behind. Ira is a genius, Father. I am learning so much from him."

"There is no need for you to work so hard," Nathan chided. "If we are short on servants, let Ira hire another. You need not grow up with dirt beneath your nails as I did. You are a young lady of means, my love." He smiled fondly at his only child.

She spread her tanned, slim-fingered hands before him. "Father, there's no dirt beneath my nails. I soaked long in the bath, and you must admit I look as fresh and pampered as any princess. During the heat of the day, while Mother rested, I lounged about and played with

Sapphire. And tried to guess your surprise." Shaina glanced sideways at her father.

"Oh, you did, did you? Well, soon your suspense will be ended, for the evening meal appears to be laid, and your mother awaits."

In a shady courtyard a slim, dark woman placed a tray of grapes and melon slices upon a table, and with a wave of her hand dismissed two servant girls who hovered nearby. Nathan embraced her warmly, and Shaina thought for the hundredth time how ardently, how obviously, he loved her mother. And with good reason, for her sultry beauty seemed only to increase with age. She was vivacious and witty, a clever companion indeed. Shaina had inherited her sea-green eyes, but otherwise she had the golden, sun-kissed look of her father's people.

When Nathan had bathed and changed into a fresh robe, they relaxed and enjoyed the flat barley bread and fruits that comprised their evening meal. It was the simple fare of Nathan's country childhood, and he preferred it still. As they ate, Shaina waited impatiently for him to mention the promised treat, but he appeared to be avoiding the subject. She sensed his reluctance to roil the serenity of the moment but could not contain her youthful curiosity. "Father, you promised my suspense would soon be ended."

Nathan hesitated a moment, then plunged nervously ahead. "In two weeks I am going to Havilah river land to visit my parents and replenish my stock of clay, but before returning, I shall travel on to view the Garden of Eden and see if I can catch a glimpse of the old patriarch, Adam, himself. They say he's aging rapidly and may not live much longer.[1] It is many miles beyond my homeland and will be a demanding journey, but it is something I have determined to do."

Nathan lapsed into silence then, seemingly lost in thought, and Shaina wondered what it all had to do with her. She wished he would finish what he had in mind. Was he planning to bring her some rare plant from his travels for her garden? What was he getting at? She glanced at her mother apprehensively, but read only disdain written upon her cool features.

Quickly, then, as though to finalize it, Nathan said, "It is my plan to take you with me."

Shaina would not have been more astounded had he said he was going to leave the potter's trade. Not even her mother ever went with him on his semiannual expeditions to acquire new supplies of clay, the journey being long and wearying. A cautious excitement began to build within her. It was a gift beyond her wildest imaginings. To walk among the rolling hills surrounding the city, and to go beyond, on and on into that mysterious land that had been her father's home before he met her mother and lost his heart and his heritage. He had told her many times about the quiet valley with giant trees spreading their limbs like leafy roofs above the dwellers. A place where sunlight filtered down upon the paths and sometimes caught the colors of gemstones lying loose along the streams and upon the ground, in secret places, where man had not snatched them up in greed.[2] Once he brought her mother an aquamarine, which he had set in a silver band. Her mother had pulled her thick black hair to one side and slid the jeweled circlet up around the dark, shining rope. The jewel was the exact color of her eyes, and she was a lovely sight, laughing there in the ivory room. Shaina had read the pleasure in her father's face as he watched her.

Now she would visit the land herself. To meet her grandparents, her uncles, her cousins. To see the riverbank where her father's servants dug the clay that became sculptures and bowls here in his workshop. Suddenly she realized she had not said a word and that her father was looking at her strangely.

"Is the idea frightening to you, child? I shall not

compel you to go, you know. It was just a whim." He sobered then. "No, Shaina, not a whim. A burning desire. I want very much to share it all with you. And I want you to make the Eden pilgrimage with me. I want it very much."

Shaina chose her words carefully. Her father had bestowed great honor upon her, and she would have him know that she understood. "I have no words to express my feelings. It is a gift beyond comprehension." Her eyes sparkled and all formality vanished. "I am more excited than I have ever been. I do not think I can survive until I am upon the back of Hadesh and headed into the hills."

"You have no idea what you are getting into," her mother snapped, "and your father has no business taking you."

Shaina sensed that a fierce battle had raged behind the scenes. It was seldom her father denied his wife anything, ever taking his greatest delight in pleasing her. But this time his wish had prevailed. At what cost Shaina could only guess.

"I am young and strong, Mother, used to hard work in the gardens. There is nothing to fear."

"And if you are attacked by robbers or wild animals, I suppose those frail young arms will hold them at bay."

Nathan spoke before his daughter could reply. "The servants are always armed, Ona. You know that. Shaina would be our first concern. And you know also my parents have a right to see their grandchild. Let this be a happy time. Anger is not appropriate here. I thought we agreed to that."

But she could not be stilled. "It's not your family you are dragging her through the wilds to see. It's that garden with the flaming swords[3] and a doddering old man who professes to have once lived there. For that you will expose her to every danger and discomfort. Don't try to fool me, Nathan. You hope to make a believer, a disciple of Adam, out of her. A fanatic who opts to live a solitary life in tents and hopes for a return to innocence.

"So devout you are, my husband! When the wealthy come and want their sacred images sculpted by your skillful hands, you cannot oblige. Oh, no, you must maintain your stupid loyalty to this invisible God who never hears, never helps, never answers. Who cannot forgive. Who locks us out of our rightful home. He's gone, Nathan. Don't you understand? Gone. Better to pray to the trees and the sun and the spirits." Ona's eyes were wet with tears. Shaina wondered if they were from anger or despair.

Nathan rose, towering over his wife as he went to her side. Ever so gently he lifted her into his arms and carried her inside. Shaina could hear the low murmur of their voices long after darkness had settled over the leafy bower where she sat. Would her mother entice him yet to leave her behind? Somehow, she thought not. This time he would stand firm. Her mother was right, of course; he *was* taking her to worship the true and living God at the gates of Eden. And if they were in time, they would hear the voice of Adam and look upon that face that had once gazed upon the face of God. Her father hadn't mentioned Eve. Was Adam's wife still alive? She would like to see her legendary beauty.

Shaina walked a bit in the gardens in an attempt to calm herself before going to her room. The fragrance of honeysuckle hung sweetly on the night air, and drifts of yellow snapdragons glowed luminous in the moonlight. When she came to her own garden, the one Ira had helped her design in a secluded corner tucked between two natural rock walls, she knelt upon the moist grass and lifted her face skyward. She did not know how to approach the great God of heaven, did not know what to say to Him, but there in the night, she felt an awareness of His presence. And—strangely—somehow a longing, a loneliness for Him.

[1] "Now the LORD God had planted a garden in the east, in Eden; and there he put the man he had formed. And the LORD God made all kinds of trees grow out of the ground—trees that were pleasing to the eye and good for food. In the middle of the garden were the tree of life and the tree of the knowledge of good and evil" (Genesis 2:8-10).

[2] "A river watering the garden flowed from Eden, and from there it divided; it had four headstreams. The name of the first is the Pishon; it winds through the entire land of Havilah, where there is gold. (The gold of that land is good; aromatic resin and onyx are also there.) The name of the second river is the Gihon; it winds through the entire land of Cush. The name of the third river is the Tigris; it runs along the east side of Asshur. And the fourth river is the Euphrates" (Genesis 2:10-14).

[3] "So the LORD God banished him from the Garden of Eden to work the ground from which he had been taken. After he drove the man out, he placed on the east side of the Garden of Eden cherubim and a flaming sword flashing back and forth to guard the way to the tree of life" (Genesis 3:23, 24).

THE JOURNEY

It was strange to be up and about so early. Shaina watched the final preparations for the journey from a small terrace below her bedchamber. She wondered impatiently if they would ever get the caravan on its way. At the moment all seemed confusion, sharp voices mingling with an occasional whinnying from some high-strung horse rebelling against a servant's prodding. The whole thing was like a dream. Men and beasts moved about in semidarkness, hazy with the mist that rose at this hour to water the earth.[1] She would always remember the moment. It was a turning point in her life, a farewell to 15 years of pampered childhood. Her father had deemed her ready. A new bond now joined them. For once he had stood his ground for her. She heard him calling her from within the house, where he had gone to bid her mother farewell. It was always a hard moment, made doubly so this time by the unpleasantness between them.

As she entered their sleeping quarters she saw tears in her father's dark eyes. He brushed a final kiss against his wife's hair and hurriedly left the room. A coolness about her mother, standing regal as a queen in the light of the flickering clay lamps, told Shaina she had not forgiven him. For just a moment the girl longed to end the tension—to say she would not go. But some deep inner awareness warned her that this was a suffering she and her father must pass through and that they must not falter.

Embraced in her mother's arms, the girl marveled

again at her silky, flowery essence. Would she ever be such a woman herself, so feminine, so powerful in her loveliness? She realized how much she was going to miss her mother. Not even Phenice, her maid since babyhood, could provide the security she felt in Ona's arms. "I will think of you here each day, Mother, and it will comfort me when the way is hard."

"And it *will* be hard, Shaina. You can be sure of that. But Phenice will be beside you. That relieves my mind a bit. And your father would lay down his life for you. Speak freely to him of your needs. He will be busy and preoccupied, but it is his desire to make this trip a delight for you." She sighed. "Shaina, Nathan has strange secret longings that I do not pretend to understand." She had never called him Nathan to her daughter before, and the girl realized they were talking woman to woman in a new way. "I love him and often make him extremely happy, but I have also robbed him of something vital to his very being. It makes me angry that I cannot fully satisfy him." A wry smile flickered across her face. "Most men would think me quite enough. But not Nathan. Sometimes I fear he hates me because he is my prisoner. But all this is too much for your young head. Go, my darling, and discover the world. I'll be waiting for you here. If you see the beautiful one, tell her I hope her piece of fruit was worth the cost." Her bitter laughter followed Shaina out into the morning light. The girl wished that they had parted on a different note.

As she got upon the back of Hadesh her heart beat with excitement. Phenice, already mounted beside her, spoke with an unusual tremor in her voice. "Will we ever see it all again, child, this civilized city and our beautiful home here?"

"You forget, Phenice, that this city is far from civilized. We dare not leave our home at night, and sometimes the evil ones pound upon our very doors.[2] Frankly, I'll take the wilderness any day. They say most animals will keep their distance if not attacked. Besides, I believe the God of heaven will go with us."

Phenice, a strong, vital woman, well over 500 years old, snorted indignantly and fondled a small silver figure that hung on a leather cord about her neck. Shaina had her own opinion of the various gods her people worshiped. Their representations and images didn't seem capable of much help to her practical mind, but she knew the servants set great store upon their powers. Even her mother knelt daily before an exquisite silver goddess rising from the foliage in her sleeping chamber.

Nathan rode up beside her, touching her shoulder lightly. "We are about to start. Shaina, I need to know God will be with us on this journey. This is so much more to me than an expedition for clay. Could we pray together?"

Shaina bowed her head, and there before the watching, wondering, impatient servants, Nathan lifted his voice to heaven in plea to God for His presence and His protection.[3] The girl heard an oath and an undercurrent of disapproval, but Nathan was a kind and generous master, and she knew the men would think long before leaving him.

"Is this your custom, Father?" she asked as he turned to ride back along the line of wagons, heavily loaded donkeys, and mounted men.

"No." He shook his head, smiling ruefully. "Usually, I am a coward."

That night they pitched their tents among the hills surrounding the city. All day they had traveled a mountain road, the ascent gentle but definite. Shaina and Phenice had looked backward in awe as the city fell beneath them. Now, in their own tent, pitched beneath a solitary pine, they looked down upon the faint lights of the valley. Shaina thought of her mother there alone. It had been a pleasant day, and they had made good progress. The men were in high spirits. Such trips were a break in routine to which they looked forward with keen anticipation.

Once in the night Shaina woke to a terrible crashing in the underbrush and, lifting the edge of her tent, saw three of the men on guard seize torches from the fire and head toward the sound, which receded into the night. *So it is true. There really are fearsome animals out there in the forest.* She shivered a little and pulled her pallet closer to Phenice.

The days ahead astounded her. She thought she had seen beauty as she and Ira had toiled in the gardens, but nothing had prepared her for trees that seemed to brush the very clouds and flowers that sprawled in profusion along the sun-dappled path. There was a lavender cupped flower, big as her father's clay bowls, with long, deep, purple stamen, ending in black, lacy disks that bobbed gently in every breeze. Shaina had to dismount and bury her face in its deep, purple throat. She begged her father to dig one for her garden, but he reminded her it would never survive the long journey, and he promised they would stop on the return trip. It seemed they encountered new wonders around every bend, and she was forever falling behind and then racing to catch up. When she stopped, two of the servants always waited as she lifted a blossom to her nose or examined some new shrub tucked into a rocky crevice. She realized her father had anticipated her curiosity and made provision for her safety.

* * * * *

By the time, six days later, they topped a ridge at evening and looked down upon Havilah river land, she felt drunk with discovery. She had beheld colors before unimagined, and breathed air as pure as crystal. The fragrance of a thousand flowers had tantalized her nostrils.

When they had made camp and eaten, all gathered

about the fire, and Nathan took out his harp. The men leaned against trees or sprawled upon the ground in relaxed anticipation. His fingers drew from the strings a sweet, plaintive tune familiar to Shaina from her childhood. It was a song of his homeland, and he played it here, tonight, as he rested upon the very borders of that beloved valley. There was a haunting quality to the music, intensified by firelight, sparks drifting upward in the leafy darkness. He had told her once that there were words to the song, words that told of Adam's sorrow upon his dismissal from Eden, and tonight she felt the sadness in her very bones.[4] Even the jovial Phenice sat quiet and sober when the last strains lingered about them.

The men called then for livelier tunes, and Nathan obliged, shaking off his nostalgia. They laughed and sang, rowdy in their freedom and their anticipation of the morrow. Usually, Shaina loved their rough voices against the soft twanging of her father's harp, and most of all she loved to watch his sandy head bent over the instrument, his strong, sure hand drawing the sounds tenderly from the strings. But tonight she could not shake the mood of the old melody. It still trembled in her heart like the first tears ever shed. How could a few musical notes recreate the exquisite pain of loss? She wondered who had created the song and how he had evoked such intensity of suffering.

Tomorrow she would meet her grandfather, and later perhaps Adam. If only they were in time!

As they descended the hillside next morning Nathan rode beside his daughter, pointing out the landmarks of his boyhood. A cluster of tents sprawled in a clearing, beyond which large fenced areas contained portions of her grandfather's vast herds. Cropland, green and lush in the morning sun, stretched to the southeast.

"Grandfather must be wealthy," Shaina exclaimed. "You never told me that."

"In his way, yes, I suppose he is, though wealth is of little consequence here. He likes what he does and does it well. And God prospers."

The river needed no identification. It meandered, serene and shining, through flowered meadows, then roared over rocks and down waterfalls, only to disappear into deep forests and out again some miles distant. The valley, in fact, seemed only a setting for this aquatic jewel, and Shaina drew the scene into her mind, detail by detail, that she might engrave it there forever. It did not surprise her, this valley. She had felt the essence of it within her always. "I too have come home, Father," she said almost reverently, hoping he would understand.

"I know," he replied, reaching for her hand. "You are a child of this place. That's why I had to bring you, no matter what your mother said. I owed it to you."

Without further conversation, they rode slowly down the hillside, closer in spirit than they had ever been. As the caravan halted before the tent settlement, a woman came from the main dwelling. Over 400 years old and nearly as tall as Nathan, she stood, golden as a sun goddess, smiling up at her son in welcome. Her hair, the color of ripe wheat, nearly the same hue as her skin, was pulled back from her face and coiled in a loose, thick knot at the back of her neck. Everything about her bespoke health and vitality, plus a peace the girl had never seen on a human face. "Nathan, my son, we've been awaiting your arrival for days. We knew the clay would bring you sooner or later. Get down, lad. I need a hug."

Nathan dismounted and held his mother in his arms a long moment, and Shaina saw, over her father's shoulder, her grandmother wipe tears from her dark eyes. Somehow, she had never thought of her father as somebody's son. Now she recognized the strong ties between them and realized that her own beautiful mother must have brought incredible sorrow to this golden woman of Havilah.

Finally Nathan turned and, beckoning to Shaina, spoke to his mother. "I have brought you a surprise. This is my daughter, my treasure, my only child. Shaina, meet Abigail, your grandmother." The girl slid from the horse and looked into those sharp, appraising eyes, knowing they were taking her measure. She did not flinch, but stared steadily back through her mother's sea-green ones. Abigail reached at last for Shaina's tanned hands and said, "These are working hands, not those of an idle city girl."

"Shaina is a determined gardener who refuses to sit in the shade and wear fine clothes. I guess her mother is more tolerant of her digging than I am. I keep telling myself I've provided well, and my daughter need not weed with the gardener, but Ona says, 'Let her be if it makes her happy.' So when other girls are romping at the baths or giggling in the grape arbors, she's setting out plants with Ira like any Havilah girl."

Shaina paid no attention to his words. She heard the pride in his voice instead. And so did his mother. Abigail put her arms around the girl and hugged her as thoroughly as she had her son. "Welcome home, sweet one. I've always feared I'd die without ever laying eyes on Nathan's daughter, but here you are as lovely as a river lily. I may never let you take her back, you know," she warned, glancing toward her son. "I've never had a daughter, and I can tell I am going to like it."

"I promised Ona she would return with us," Nathan cautioned, thinking, Shaina felt sure, of those last troubled moments at home. "But we'll spend a few days here, and that will give you time in which to get acquainted."

"A few days? It will take the men at least two weeks to dig and dry the clay. Then there's the loading of the wagons. What is this foolishness about a few days?"

"I have other plans, Mother, which I will share at the evening meal. They will be of interest to you. Where is Father?"

"He is bringing in sheep from the river grazing lands. Why don't you ride out to meet him? Just be careful not to startle the sheep."

"You're talking to an old shepherd boy. Do you really think I'd ride head-on into a flock?"

Abigail shrugged. "You've been a long time away, Nathan. Who knows what the city has done to you?"

"It has made me ever lonelier for the simplicity and peace of this land. You could never imagine the evil that thrives elsewhere in the world."

"Have they no fear of God?" Abigail asked.

Her son snorted. "God is but the victim of their scorn and ridicule. They laugh in His face and plot new mischief to flaunt their imperviousness to His wrath." [5]

"Surely you defend Him, Nathan, and speak of His love." Her eyes rested upon him, awaiting his answer, but he did not return her glance.

"No, Mother, I do not," he said after a pause. "It would mean the loss of my business, my wife, and perhaps my life, and I'm not really in much of a position to come to God's defense at any rate."

Shaina wished she had not heard his reply, that her grandmother had not asked the question. Her father mounted his horse, and wheeling abruptly about, headed down the road.

Entering the tent, Abigail set about to prepare a meal with the help of two servant girls. As she poured rice into a pot, Shaina watched curiously. Occasionally her mother served a tray of drink or fruits, but the actual preparation she left to their servants.

"Shaina, would you gather some greens from the cooking garden behind the tent?" Abigail handed her a cutting tool and a basket. Reluctant to admit her ignorance, the girl hesitated.

"I'm afraid I might cut the wrong thing, Grandmother. I've grown only flowers."

Abigail turned the cooking pot over to a servant and motioned for her granddaughter to follow her. Behind the tent she entered a large garden boasting an astonishing array of fruits and vegetables. It made Shaina's mouth water just to walk up and down the rows. At home the servants purchased all their food in the marketplace, and she knew nothing of the intricacies of raising raspberries and carrots. But the gardener in her responded, and she listened with excitement as her grandmother pointed out the various plants and spoke of their needs and habits. Together they filled the bowl with huge, ruffled, green leaves, and Abigail lifted the overlap of her plain brown robe in which to gather ripe pears. They spent a long time in the garden, and it was only because of the faithful girls gathered about the fire tending the kettle and adding vegetables,[6] that the meal was prepared when Nathan and Sepp arrived in a cloud of dust with the sheep.

Later, seated about a generous table, they talked as the sun slipped behind the ridge. The food had been a wonder to Shaina. The wild brown river rice, garnished with carrots and onions from Abigail's garden, had been delicious. She had watched a servant girl crumble small bits of greens into the bubbling pot, and Abigail had explained that they were herbs and that tomorrow she would show her where they grew in a sheltered corner by the cooking tent. So much to learn and only a few days! She nibbled on a crusty hunk of dark rye bread and tried to decide what she thought of goat's milk. Sepp had looked at her shrewdly and said simply, "You are welcome in this place, child of Nathan." No hug. No touch. Yet Shaina felt his satisfaction at her presence. He was someone to anticipate, to savor slowly, to win.

As they ate the juicy pears with a mild, soft cheese, Abigail turned to her son. "Let us hear the plan that is so important that you must drag my granddaughter away before I even know her."

Nathan sat a moment, biting the last bits of fruit from its core, weighing his words. He was as uncomfortable, Shaina thought, as he had been when telling her mother, but for very different reasons. With Ona he was the pure one, always accusing her indifference with his loneliness for God. Here, he was the sinner, the one who walked away, who sold out, who rejected God. Ona scorned his longings to see the world's beginnings, while those around this table would not understand his ambiguous loyalties. Her heart went out to him. For the first time she realized, as his daughter, that there would be choices for her, too. The thought made her uneasy.

"I have long desired to see for myself the Garden of Eden, and to meet, if possible, the patriarch Adam. I have heard from passing caravans in the city that he is aging, and I dared not wait longer. Who knows, perhaps when he dies, the great God of heaven will whisk the garden away and we will have no reminder of how it all began." A hint of banter in his voice masked the terrible hunger of his heart.

"It's a long journey," Sepp said, "and there are cities where one hardly dares camp within or without the walls. Why not leave Shaina here with us if you insist upon going? It is no experience for a child."

The girl held her breath. She wanted to go, but dared not say so in the presence of this giant of a man who seemed something of a patriarch himself.

Before Nathan could answer, Abigail spoke. "I will go with you, Nathan and care for the girl. It has ever been my dream. I'm in the prime of life and have no fears. We will take a few strong and trusted servants, keep our party small, and travel quickly."

Shaina glanced cautiously at her grandfather to see how he was reacting to her suggestion, but his weathered face was inscrutable.

"You are needed here, Mother," Nathan said. "There are a hundred tasks a day demanding your time and talents, though God knows it would take a great burden from my mind, and I am grateful for your offer."

"Let her go." Her husband's voice was firm and final. "She has worked hard and deserves her dream."

"But if anything should happen, if I did not return her to this place, I could never forgive myself."

"When she dies, it will be the will of God whether here or there, and your mother will not die easily anywhere." Sepp chuckled and placed his hand over his wife's. "She is a woman of many resources."

Shaina could remain still no longer. "Then it's settled? You will go, Grandmother? Oh, this is better than I imagined. Let's leave Phenice here. She's uneasy away from the city and dreads journeying further."

Abigail smiled at her granddaughter's enthusiasm. "There may be days, child, when you wish you had her along. If we take no female servants, you must help with all the food preparations and washing of garments. You will learn a bit about the life of a servant and may never again dispense so readily with faithful Phenice."

"I want you to think carefully about this, Mother." Nathan rose from the table. "It is enough that I endanger my daughter's life without putting you at risk."

"You cannot know how I have often longed to see that spot where Adam walked in perfect unity with his Creator, and, God willing, to see him, too. I hear they have been ridiculed and accused and harassed over all these years. What a price they have paid!"

"What a price we have all paid," Shaina said softly, echoing her mother's bitterness. Her words did not escape Abigail.

"To walk with God is a privilege we all have, Shaina, and when it is over we will forget the suffering and remember only what it cost Him." [7]

"I don't understand it all, Grandmother."

"Nor do I. I simply trust Him. Once our ancestor Seth, third son of Adam, traveled through this valley and taught us. He said, 'Just trust God. He loves you and has promised to make all things right.' So that's what we've done, Sepp and I, just trusted Him. Sometimes when I'm working in the garden I feel His presence so close that I can almost reach out and touch Him."

"But if we are all sinners, how will anything ever change? How will God ever accept us again?"

"Seth said God made a promise there in the garden that day when Eve ate the fruit, and while no one understands it totally, it is a promise of hope. An oath by God that He will send a Deliverer.[8] I guess every woman who believes it looks at her first male child and wonders if he will be the one."

"Did you think that about my father?"

"He was a good baby and a gentle child. The kind of son every mother enjoys, especially after raising a few rascals. Of all my sons, Shaina, he seemed most fitted to become a deliverer. They are all sons of God, now, the rascals, and only Nathan, my precious Nathan, walks apart from Him." Tears stood in Abigail's eyes, and she could speak no more.

Shaina bent and dropped a kiss on her grandmother's shining hair as she still sat at the table. "Let us go in, for it's getting cool. And don't grieve over Father. Surely he would not be making this pilgrimage if he had abandoned God. He speaks to me often of Him. There are images of gods everywhere at home, but Father has always taught me that they are useless hunks of metal, however beautiful, and that there is only one true God, who lives beyond the skies and who knows our thoughts and longs for our love and obedience."

"You are right. A spark still flickers in his heart. We have three days in which to make our preparations for this journey, and we must work fiercely. Then we will rest and worship on the Sabbath, and set out on first day." [9] Shaina had no idea what Sabbath was, but decided she'd asked enough questions for one day.

When Abigail said "work," she meant a whirlwind of activity totally beyond Shaina's experience. The two washed clothing and hung them on bushes to dry, baked flat, hard breads, and packed supplies of legumes and dried fruit in goatskin bags. Shaina dug and scrubbed root vegetables and tied barley in small pouches.

Late on sixth day, the preparations dwindled to a total standstill, and by the time the sun hung like one of Abigail's ripe apricots over the ridge, the entire clan had gathered at tables among the orchard trees with a simple meal before them.[10] Over the past few days Shaina had met an occasional uncle or cousin, but such had been her concentration upon the journey that she had had no time to appraise her relatives. Now they were gathered here, well over 400 of them, in a spirit of something between celebration and worship. Shaina, seated beside Nathan, sensed they were waiting for something. When the last child was settled, Sepp stood. Still he waited, until all sound ceased. Then he spoke to the men, women, children, and servants seated before him.

"Another Sabbath is ours. God be praised for His goodness and protection. For Nathan's safe arrival. And for the Promised One." Taller than her father, he stood like a giant among his family and friends, yet she sensed a reverent humility in her grandfather.

"What is *Sabbath?*" she whispered to her father, but he laid his finger over his lips in warning. She had not noticed before the pile of stones carefully arranged beside her grandfather. Her mind was bursting with questions. Suddenly a servant picked up a handsome lamb and placed it in Sepp's hands, where with one deft stroke her grandfather slew it. It happened so fast that the girl could only gasp in horror. It was all she could do not to scream. Had he gone mad? She begged Nathan with her eyes for answers, but his lips mouthed only the word *Wait.*

His hands dripping blood, Sepp placed the lamb on the altar of stones and set fire to it with a torch held by a waiting servant. The stench of burning flesh drifted down across the tables, and Shaina thought she would be sick. Her grandfather bowed his massive head and prayed, but she could barely focus her mind upon his words, though she did hear him mention again the Promised One. Even after he finished his prayer, all sat with bowed heads praying silently. Only gradually did subdued conversation flow once more about them.[11]

As she ate, she whispered to her father. "Why did he do it? It was awful. It spoiled this whole lovely time. Why are all of the people so relaxed, as though they have nothing on earth to do?"

Nathan sighed, knowing he should have prepared her. "Shaina, it all has deep meaning, but this is not the time to discuss it. While we are traveling toward Eden, your grandmother will answer your questions. From now until tomorrow night at sundown, there will be no work done in this place. It is a time for the worship of God, for communion with Him. It is His command.[12] We'll talk more about it later. Now, eat, my love, and no more heavy thoughts." Nathan bit into an apple with his strong, white teeth and the juice spurted in a fine spray. Shaina knew there'd be no more answers this night.

* * * * *

For six days they had been traveling through the deep forest, having long since left the meadows of Havilah behind. Sepp had decided it was far too dangerous for them to take the road passing through the cities of the lowlands. There men vied for the traveler's body and his goods, and it was the rare caravan that passed through without loss of life or property. Instead he drew upon his splendid memory to find a trail through the hills used years before by his forefathers. He sent with them Reuben, his best scout. Even so, it would be a challenging journey, and now Nathan and Reuben rode ahead, ever alert, sweeping the forest with cautious, searching eyes. Abigail and Shaina followed, and behind rode four menservants, tall and strong as oaks, for their protection. A few beasts of burden, loaded with supplies, straggled in their wake.

"Only eight of us against the danger," Shaina had said as they mounted their horses the first morning.

"Nine," Abigail corrected. "God goes before and in the midst of us. Never forget that." The entire clan had gathered about them, and Sepp had prayed solemnly for their safety and for the success of their mission.

Now, the towering trees had given way at last to a clearing, and they followed the sandy shores of a long lake. Sunlight shimmered through the clear, green water to glint on pebbles of gold far below. Shaina begged her father to stop and make camp in this place of light and wonder. They had pushed at a hard pace, so Nathan, knowing his mother needed time to prepare for Sabbath, called a halt. A long, lithe lion strode along the shoreline, his muscles rippling beneath his golden hide. Shaina's heart hammered in her chest, but the beast turned away from them and headed into the underbrush. Nathan, erecting the small tent in which Shaina and Abigail slept, sensed the fear in his daughter. "Here, where man seldom comes, they simply keep their distance. It's only where they've been hunted and killed that they become vicious."

After they had all enjoyed a refreshing swim, the men stretched out upon the sand, letting the sun bake into their tired bodies. Shaina and Abigail sat on a flat ledge, dangling their feet in the water and attempting to identify the exotic flowers blooming about them. Twirling a shaggy, yellow blossom in one hand, the girl gathered her courage and blurted out, "Why did Grandfather burn the lamb?"

The woman smiled, sunlight playing across her strong, tanned features. "I wondered if your father had explained that to you. It's indeed a strange act if you don't know its meaning.

"Remember, I told you about the Promised One. Well, Seth said, 'He must die. He must shed His blood for our sins.' It's all a great mystery, but God wants us to take it seriously, to be aware of the terrible price of sin, so He's instructed us to kill a sheep, a perfect sheep, because it represents the One who must die, and to burn it on the altar. Each time we know it is our sin that brings death to the innocent lamb, but far worse, to One who comes.[13]

"Your grandfather offers a lamb for our encampment every sixth day at sundown, when the Sabbath begins.[14] Even though I've seen him do it hundreds of times, my heart yet stands still at the awful act and its significance."

"Did it cover my sins, too, the lamb that Grandfather killed, or only those of you who are followers of God?"

"When the Promised One comes, Shaina, He will die for all. Some will accept His sacrifice, and some will scoff and deny Him. If you believe and obey, it is for you." [15]

"I have another question for you, Grandmother." Shaina sloshed her feet idly in the warm, clear water. "I do not understand Sabbath. Why is the seventh day any different from the rest?"

"Has your father told you nothing? In your home, is there no reverence for Sabbath?" Abigail looked at her in astonishment.

Knowing the sorrow she inflicted, the girl shook her head.

Her grandmother sighed heavily. "When God finished creating the earth, my child—all this beauty here before us—He liked what He had done. Just as you and I look over our gardens after a day's work and we are pleased. He'd been six days at His wondrous activity, and He declared the seventh a period of rest and rejoicing. A time to enjoy His new creations and for them to enjoy Him. God called it Sabbath, and He made a simple rule—that we too were to rest and rejoice on that day. No work. Only fellowship with Him." [16]

"That's lovely. Just lovely," Shaina breathed. "Oh, I wish I'd known before. Why did Father never tell me?"

Her grandmother took her hand and they sat in the sunny silence, content in their new closeness, until at last Abigail rose and awakened a servant to start a fire. "We must cook something for the morrow, Shaina, and we shall celebrate the Sabbath here in this beautiful place. It seems Eden itself couldn't have been lovelier."

Later, in the darkness by the fire, Shaina asked her father, "Why did you never speak of Sabbath and show us how to observe it?"

Her father laughed bitterly. "Your mother has no patience with such acts of worship, and her sacred images would bang their silver heads together at the very thought of God's presence in the house. It's two separate worlds, little one, and in marrying your mother I made my choice. I brought you here so you could make yours." His words birthed in her, once again, a nagging uneasiness.

Two weeks later the little party followed a wide, eager stream out of the hills and into the valley of Eden. They had cautiously skirted an area inhabited by giants,[17] lost their way for a period of three days, and seen strange, enormous beasts that could have trampled them easily into the loam of the forest floor had they been so inclined. The men cheered lustily as they left the forest behind.

"Instead of making all that racket, Nathan, we might better thank the God of heaven for bringing us safely to our destination," Abigail scolded, riding up beside her son.

"You are quite right, my mother." Nathan gathered the little band about him, and they prayed quietly on the green hillside, the horses knee-deep in sweet-smelling grasses. As the rim of hills curved downward toward the valley, great white cliffs cupped an expanse of land, shielding it completely from view.

"That," Reuben spoke reverently, "is the garden."

"It's huge." Shaina heard the surprise in her grandmother's voice. "I always pictured it more the size of our acreage at home."

"They say it's a three-day journey to ride the length of it. And at every point the cliffs prevent entrance, except at the gates. In my boyhood my father told me much about this valley." Reuben's eyes followed the white walls. "I never dreamed I'd have the chance to behold it with my own eyes."

"Nor I," Abigail echoed softly.

A large encampment, a mile or two distant, spread toward the foothills of another elevated region, and Shaina guessed it to be the home of the patriarch Adam, the father of them all. They ate on the hillside, savoring the moment, hardly aware of the dry wheat rounds and figs that they consumed. Each traveler busy with his own thoughts, they spoke few words.

When at last they moved on, Shaina rode beside her father, wishing to share the experience with him. They followed the cliffs for several hours, coming at last to a trail leading downward onto the valley floor. In the growing dusk a strange light flickered upon the dirt path, yet the sun had long since slipped behind the trees.

"What is it?" Shaina asked uneasily, but no one answered, for no one knew. Only as they reached level ground at the foot of the cliff could they see, up ahead, the most breathtaking sight any of them would ever experience. Before the entrance to Eden two beings stood, awesome in their size and beauty.[18] Their wings arched over a focal point between them. From it blazed a flashing, turning light, alive with the glory of God, laying fingers of red-gold fire across the darkening sky, the shadowed earth, and the trembling hearts of Nathan's little band. They slid from their horses and fell to the ground in terror. Nothing had prepared them for the sight. Was God angry at their presence? Were they trespassing upon sacred ground? Would they die? With that glory slicing into her, exposing her inner being, Shaina suddenly recoiled from the selfishness she sensed there. Every petulant or dishonest word she'd ever spoken now shouted in her memory. For the first time she knew every vice of which she was capable. She was sin itself. During what seemed an eternity she wept into the black, fertile earth of Eden valley until she felt a hand upon her shoulder, gently lifting her, turning her away from the Light. "Come, child, you won't die, at least not now, not from this Light." The voice urged the others to their feet and led them, stumbling like blind men, some distance from the angels and that soul-searing glory.

"What is it?" Shaina voiced again the question she'd asked earlier upon the path.

"It's the presence of God guarding the gate," the woman said quietly, as though she'd repeated it a thousand times before. Only then did Shaina look at her and know instantly she was Eve, the mother of mankind—or the betrayer of mankind, as Ona liked to call her. Shaina had expected a bent and wrinkled old crone. But what she saw was an ageless face, startling in its beauty, heart-wrenching in its sorrow, yet at the same time glowing with a steady peace. She could have stared at it forever.

Nathan spoke in his gentle way. "Thank you for coming to us. It's a very frightening experience to stumble upon that splendor. You must be Eve. We have traveled many miles to view the garden and to meet you and Adam. We did not mean to inconvenience you."

Eve laughed, and the sound was silvery, like a small waterfall in moonlight. "Can you imagine how many terrified people I've dragged away from that spot? Though not many anymore. The scorners are all busy with their evil schemes, and the worshipers grow few. Feel free to spend the night anywhere in the valley. You are safe here. I brought you food." She placed a warm loaf in Abigail's hands and a bowl of lentil stew in Shaina's. "We watched you, Adam and I, as you skirted the walls this afternoon."

Before they could express their gratitude, she'd slipped into the darkness. Almost wordlessly they made camp and ate, as though that holy Light had struck them dumb. Even now it flashed and flickered across the walls of Shaina's tent despite the fact that they had pitched it some distance away from the entrance to Eden.

"Grandmother," she whispered softly, "this is a sacred place." But Abigail slept and made no reply. Shaina slipped quietly from the tent and knelt facing the Light. She did not know why she did so, and even the day before the thought of doing so would have surprised her. But now it seemed to be the right thing to do. Words rushed to her lips. "O mighty God," she said, "I am a sinner—I realize that now. I share in the rebellion of my race. But I believe in the Promised One. Somehow I know that You will speak to me. Teach me what You desire of me."

* * * * *

When morning sun gilded the valley, creeping over the pastures and fields of Adam and Seth's extended properties, the Light did not seem so menacing. Soon after breakfast, Shaina was begging to visit Adam's encampment.

"You can't just go and stare at them like curiosities, my love," Nathan cautioned. "It is a little awkward unless they invite us."

But she pleaded so ardently that her father succumbed, and she set off alone toward the sounds of bleating sheep and human voices. She came upon a path bordered with shrubs and bright clumps of scarlet flowers, obviously all tended with loving care, and as her eyes were riveted upon their beauty, a figure headed toward her.

"Do you like them? They are Adam's favorites," the woman said cheerfully.

Startled, Shaina looked again into that face unparalleled in beauty, warm with kindness, and at this moment touched with a hint of humor. Before she could answer, Eve went on.

"I thought you would come early, so I walked over to meet you. You have the impatience of youth and—I have sensed—a heart hungry for God. Come, I want to show you Adam's gardens. My husband is eager to meet you. He does not go to the fields much anymore. There are younger ones for that. But he loves his flowers."

"I can't believe I am here with you." The girl looked at her companion in awe.

"Remember, Shaina—is not that what your father called you?—Adam and I are sinners in need of the Promised One's blood. In fact, we are chief among sinners, for we walked and talked with God and still doubted Him. Or at least I did. Do not look at me with wonder. I want you to understand, before you leave, the tragedy that happened here."

They left the shadowed path and entered the most exquisite gardens Shaina had ever laid eyes upon. Roses, cleverly pruned and trained, bloomed everywhere against backdrops of evergreen and dark glossy shrubs. Areas of soft, green grass broke the profusion of color, and fountains splashed into clear pools. Shaina sucked in her breath and held it. She had a wild, impossible wish that Ira might stand beside her to see this wonder.

A tower of a man spoke from a height well beyond her grandfather's. "You are a lover of beauty. It is written all over your face, my daughter. Welcome. Let me show you around."

I am his daughter, Shaina thought in wonder. *Bone of his bone, flesh of his flesh.* Impulsively, she laid her young cheek against his mighty arm, and he smiled with delight and gave her a warm hug. He did not look so old, but his steps were slow and deliberate, where once she knew they had been quick and sure. As he showed her each plant and spoke of its habits and needs, she heard no hint of age in his voice—only interest and enthusiasm.

"You have reproduced the garden here in all its glory, haven't you?" Shaina asked eagerly at last.

"Oh, child," he spoke hurriedly, as though to dispel her error quickly, "you are mistaken. It is true I have tried, but here with the weeds and the insects to destroy, there is no comparison. Remember also," and he smiled sadly, "God created *that* garden. Man cannot make another like it." [19]

They sat on a bench by a pool where ruffled white irises bent above their own reflections in the water. A butterfly, purple and blue and big as Adam's broad hand, flitted from flower to flower. A question burned in Shaina's mind, and nothing could have restrained her from asking it. "Last night, when I was lying before the Light, I was aware of all my—what do you call it?—sinfulness. It was terrible. I felt unclean in the presence of that Light—in the presence of God. I felt my utter inability ever to become pure enough to walk with God as His friend the way you two did in Eden. [20] Even if the Promised One dies, how will we ever again become clean and fit for His presence?"

"We do not fully understand it all ourselves, Shaina," Adam replied thoughtfully. "God's ways will always be a mystery to us to some extent, but it seems the Promised One's blood pays the debt.[21] When there is sin, death must always result.[22] Eternal death, a terrible, total separation from God. The Promised One will die that death for us. But He will do more if we allow Him. He will move into our very flesh and minds until His purity becomes our purity, and we are clean once again.[23] It is not an easy process, and it requires cooperation and submission on our part, and a certain hunger for Him. It is long and painful, and yet joyful at the same time. We might throw away all we've gained in a moment of weakness, but we can place ourselves all over again, beaten and despairing, in His hands, and cling to His mercy. Are you brave, child, brave enough?"

"I don't know," Shaina admitted honestly. "My mother is a worshiper of images, and my father—well, my father is a believer, but he is not brave."

"We will pray for you," Eve assured kindly, placing her arm about Shaina. "When we offer sacrifice before the Light, we will pray for you."

Later, Adam took them all once again around the gardens and dug bulbs for Shaina and Abigail to carry home. In the evening they sat about a table heaped with the bounties of Adam's fields and Abigail's sacks. Carefully she'd guarded the rich, dried fruits and plump nuts she'd packed as gifts. As they ate, Adam spoke of the early years after they had to leave the garden. They'd had no tools and no knowledge, and only by trial and error had they tamed the wilderness.[24]

"That was not all," Eve added, remembering. "There were the taunts of others, our own flesh and blood, their anger at our failure. Our children and grandchildren ridiculed and threatened us. Sometimes we feared for our lives. And they hated God. Perhaps that is why they began to worship gods from their own imaginations—

gods that they did not hate and fear."

"Even that was not the worst," Adam said steadily. "The death of Abel, that was the worst of all, but she cannot speak of that." [25]

All these hundreds of years, Shaina thought, as she glanced at Eve's haunted eyes, *and the pain is still fresh. Perhaps one never recovers from that first encounter with death."*

"But here we are talking of sorrows, when there is much over which to rejoice." Adam turned the conversation briskly toward God's precious promise and the long-awaited Deliverer. "No matter how long we wait, He *will* come. Remember that, my friends, even after I sleep in the good earth. I do not dread the end. We have known terrible pain these many years as we've watched death invade the planet. Sin has engulfed our children, and our children's children, and we've drunk the cup of guilt to its bitter dregs. Over and over we've pleaded for our descendants to humble themselves before God, only to have them laugh in our faces or scream accusations at us. No, death holds no fears for us. Am I correct, my darling?"

Eve, smiling at him wistfully, took his hand and nodded.

Shaina understood then that no garden, however beautiful, could ever erase the agony they had endured, and her own heart ached in sympathy.

"We've tried to help our descendants understand," Eve explained, sadly, her voice a whisper, "that God's sorrow over our loss exceeds our own."

"You can't imagine," she continued, eyes lighting, "what it was like to be with Him, to find Him suddenly beside you in the evening, to feel the power of His presence burning into your soul before He was even visible. He took such pleasure in our excitement over each newly discovered wonder of His creation. Turning sometimes, I'd catch the pure delight in His eyes as He watched us, and I felt cherished and safe and content.

"I know the pain I have caused Him all these years." Her voice broke. "And the price it will cost Him. I miss Him. Always I miss Him. And to hear Him cursed and taunted, my Precious Friend, by my own flesh and blood—it's almost more than I can bear."

"A few have heeded our words," Adam comforted, placing his arm about her, but in his face Shaina read such suffering as she had never seen upon a human countenance. "Man born into sinfulness no longer finds the things of God appealing. It requires a long, slow miraculous turning to bring him once more into tune with His Maker, and few will submit to the process because it is so much easier to simply enjoy the bounties of the earth and gratify every impulse. And upon us both rests the burden of this knowledge—the sordidness of man, his cruelty, his greed. All our legacy to those for whom God planned so much."

Nathan picked up his harp and softly, in the darkness with the Light playing over the table and the sober faces surrounding it, plucked that old haunting melody from the strings. To their amazement, Eve began to sing, the story of loss and sorrow flowing effortlessly from her lips. Her clear, sweet voice, trembling now and then, wove about the music like a garland of flowers. When Nathan laid down the harp, there was only the sound of weeping, and Shaina knew it was from Eve herself whence the song had sprung.

[1] "This is the account of the heavens and the earth when they were created.

"When the LORD God made the earth and the heavens, no shrub of the field had yet appeared on the earth and no plant of the field had yet sprung up; the LORD God had not sent rain on the earth and there was no man to work the ground, but streams came up from the earth and watered the whole surface of the ground" (Genesis 2:4-6).

[2] "Now the earth was corrupt in God's sight and was full of violence" (Genesis 6:11).

[3] "And pray in the Spirit on all occasions with all kinds of prayers and requests. With this in mind, be alert and always keep on praying for all the saints" (Ephesians 6:18).

"I want men everywhere to lift up holy hands in prayer, without anger or disputing" (1 Timothy 2:8).

"The prayer of a righteous man is powerful and effective" (James 5:19).

[4] "So the LORD God banished him from the Garden of Eden to work the ground from which he had been taken" (Genesis 3:23).

[5] "The LORD saw how great man's wickedness on the earth had become, and that every inclination of the thoughts of his heart was only evil all the time. The LORD was grieved that he had made man on the earth, and his heart was filled with pain" (Genesis 6:5, 6).

[6] "Then God said, 'I give you every seed-bearing plant on the face of the whole earth and every tree that has fruit with seed in it. They will be yours for food' " (Genesis 1:29).

"The LORD God took the man and put him in the Garden of Eden to work it and take care of it. And the LORD God commanded the man, 'You are free to eat from any tree in the garden; but you must not eat from the tree of the knowledge of good and evil, for when you eat of it you will surely die' " (Genesis 2:15, 16).

[7] "He was despised and rejected by men, a man of sorrows, and familiar with suffering. Like one from whom men hide their faces he was despised, and we esteemed him not. Surely he took up our infirmities and carried our sorrows, yet we considered him stricken by God, smitten by him, and afflicted. But he was pierced for our transgressions, he was crushed for our iniquities; the punishment that brought us peace was upon him, and by his wounds we are healed" (Isaiah 53:3-5).

"Return, O Israel, to the LORD your God. Your sins have been your downfall! Take words with you and return to the LORD. Say to him: 'Forgive all our sins and receive us graciously, that we may offer the fruit of our lips' " (Hosea 14:1, 2).

[8] "And I will put enmity between you and the woman, and between your offspring and hers; he will crush your head, and you will strike his heel" (Genesis 3:15).

"For God so loved the world that he gave his one and only Son, that whoever believes in him shall not perish but have eternal life. For God did not send his Son into the world to condemn the world, but to save the world through him" (John 3:16, 17).

⁹ "And God blessed the seventh day and made it holy" (Genesis 2:3).

"Observe the Sabbath day by keeping it holy, as the LORD your God has commanded you. Six days you shall labor and do all your work, but the seventh day is a Sabbath to the LORD your God. On it you shall not do any work, neither you, nor your son or daughter, nor your manservant or maidservant, nor your ox, your donkey or any of your animals, nor the alien within your gates, so that your manservant and maidservant may rest, as you do. Remember that you were slaves in Egypt and that the LORD your God brought you out of there with a mighty hand and an outstretched arm. Therefore the LORD your God has commanded you to observe the Sabbath day" (Deuteronomy 5:12-15).

"Then he said to them, 'The Sabbath was made for man, not man for the Sabbath. So the Son of Man is Lord even of the Sabbath' " (Mark 2:27, 28).

¹⁰ "It is a sabbath of rest for you, and you must deny yourselves. From the evening of the ninth day of the month until the following evening you are to observe your sabbath" (Leviticus 23:32).

¹¹ "If he brings a lamb as his sin offering, he is to bring a female without defect. He is to lay his hand on its head and slaughter it for a sin offering at the place where the burnt offering is slaughtered. Then the priest shall take some of the blood of the sin offering with his finger and put it on the horns of the altar of burnt offering and pour out the rest of the blood at the base of the altar. He shall remove all the fat, just as the fat is removed from the lamb of the fellowship offering, and the priest shall burn it on the altar on top of the offerings made to the LORD by fire. In this way the priest will make atonement for him for the sin he has committed, and he will be forgiven" (Leviticus 4:32-35).

¹² "By the seventh day God had finished the work he had been doing; so on the seventh day he rested from all his work. And God blessed the seventh day and made it holy, because on

it he rested from all the work of creating that he had done" (Genesis 2:2, 3).

"Remember the Sabbath day by keeping it holy. Six days you shall labor and do all your work, but the seventh day is a Sabbath to the LORD your God. On it you shall not do any work, neither you, nor your son or daughter, nor your manservant or maidservant, nor your animals, nor the alien within your gates. For in six days the LORD made the heavens and the earth, the sea, and all that is in them, but he rested the seventh day. Therefore the LORD blessed the Sabbath day and made it holy" (Exodus 20:8-11).

"If you keep your feet from breaking the Sabbath and from doing as you please on my holy day, if you call the Sabbath a delight and the LORD's holy day honorable, and if you honor it by not going your own way and not doing as you please or speaking idle words, then you will find your joy in the LORD, and I will cause you to ride on the heights of the land" (Isaiah 58:13, 14).

"But if you are careful to obey me, declares the LORD, and bring no load through the gates of this city on the Sabbath, but keep the Sabbath day holy by not doing any work on it, then kings who sit on David's throne will come through the gates of this city with their officials. They and their officials will come riding in chariots and on horses, accompanied by the men of Judah and those living in Jerusalem, and this city will be inhabited forever" (Jeremiah 17:24, 25).

"He went to Nazareth, where he had been brought up, and on the Sabbath day he went into the synagogue, as was his custom. And he stood up to read" (Luke 4:16).

"From Perga they went on to Pisidian Antioch. On the Sabbath they entered the synagogue and sat down. After the reading from the Law and the Prophets, the synagogue rulers sent word to them, saying, 'Brothers, if you have a message of encouragement for the people, please speak' " (Acts 13:14, 15).

"On the Sabbath we went outside the city gate to the river, where we expected to find a place of prayer. We sat down and began to speak to the women who had gathered there" (Acts 16:13).

"As his custom was, Paul went into the synagogue, and on three Sabbath days he reasoned with them from the Scriptures, explaining and proving that the Christ had to suffer and rise from the dead. 'This Jesus I am proclaiming to you is the Christ,' he said" (Acts 17:2, 3).

"Every Sabbath he reasoned in the synagogue, trying to persuade Jews and Greeks" (Acts 18:4).

[13] "Now Abel kept flocks, and Cain worked the soil. In the course of time Cain brought some of the fruits of the soil as an offering to the LORD. But Abel brought fat portions from some of the firstborn of his flock. The LORD looked with favor on Abel and his offering, but on Cain and his offering he did not look with favor. So Cain was very angry, and his face was downcast" (Genesis 4:2-5).

"Then Noah built an altar to the LORD and, taking some of all the clean animals and clean birds, he sacrificed burnt offerings on it. The LORD smelled the pleasing aroma and said in his heart: 'Never again will I curse the ground because of man, even though every inclination of his heart is evil from childhood. And never again will I destroy all living creatures, as I have done' " (Genesis 8:20, 21).

"So Abram moved his tents and went to live near the great trees of Mamre at Hebron, where he built an altar to the LORD" (Genesis 13:18).

"Abraham looked up and there in a thicket he saw a ram caught by its horns. He went over and took the ram and sacrificed it as a burnt offering instead of his son. So Abraham called that place 'The LORD will provide.' And to this day it is said, 'On the mountain of the LORD it will be provided' " (Genesis 22:13, 14).

"So Jacob took an oath in the name of the Fear of his father Isaac. He offered a sacrifice there in the hill country and invited his relatives to a meal. After they had eaten, they spent the night there" (Genesis 31:53, 54).

"The next day John saw Jesus coming toward him and said, 'Look, the Lamb of God, who takes away the sin of the world!' " (John 1:29).

[14] "And God said, 'Let there be light,' and there was light. God saw that the light was good, and he separated the light from the darkness. God called the light 'day' and the darkness he called 'night.' And there was evening, and there was morning—the first day. . . . And there was evening, and there was morning—the second day. . . . And there was evening, and

there was morning—the third day. . . . And there was evening, and there was morning—the fourth day. . . . And there was evening, and there was morning—the fifth day. . . . God saw all that he had made, and it was very good. And there was evening, and there was morning—the sixth day" (Genesis 1:3-31).

[15] "Just as man is destined to die once, and after that to face judgment, so Christ was sacrificed once to take away the sins of many people; and he will appear a second time, not to bear sin, but to bring salvation to those who are waiting for him" (Hebrews 9:27, 28).

"The law is only a shadow of the good things that are coming—not the realities themselves. For this reason it can never, by the same sacrifices repeated endlessly year after year, make perfect those who draw near to worship. If it could, would they not have stopped being offered? For the worshipers would have been cleansed once for all, and would no longer have felt guilty for their sins. But those sacrifices are an annual reminder of sins, because it is impossible for the blood of bulls and goats to take away sins. Therefore, when Christ came into the world, he said: 'Sacrifice and offering you did not desire, but a body you prepared for me; with burnt offerings and sin offerings you were not pleased. Then I said, "Here I am—it is written about me in the scroll—I have come to do your will, O God." ' First he said, 'Sacrifices and offerings, burnt offerings and sin offerings you did not desire, nor were you pleased with them' (although the law required them to be made). Then he said, 'Here I am, I have come to do your will.' He sets aside the first to establish the second. And by that will, we have been made holy through the sacrifice of the body of Jesus Christ once for all. Therefore, brothers, since we have confidence to enter the Most Holy Place by the blood of Jesus, by a new and living way opened for us through the curtain, that is, his body, and since we have a great priest over the house of God, let us draw near to God with a sincere heart in full assurance of faith, having our hearts sprinkled to cleanse us from a guilty conscience and having our bodies washed with pure water" (Hebrews 10:1-10, 19-22).

[16] "Thus the heavens and the earth were completed in all their vast array.

"By the seventh day God had finished the work he had been

doing; so on the seventh day he rested from all his work. And God blessed the seventh day and made it holy, because on it he rested from all the work of creating that he had done" (Genesis 2:1-3).

"Remember the Sabbath day by keeping it holy. Six days you shall labor and do all your work, but the seventh day is a sabbath to the LORD your God. On it you shall not do any work, neither you, nor your son or daughter, nor your manservant or maidservant, nor your animals, nor the alien within your gates. For in six days the LORD made the heavens and the earth, the sea, and all that is in them, but he rested on the seventh day. Therefore the LORD blessed the Sabbath day and made it holy" (Exodus 20:8-11).

"Then the LORD said to Moses, 'Say to the Israelites, "You must observe my Sabbaths. This will be a sign between me and you for the generations to come, so you may know that I am the LORD, who makes you holy" ' " (Exodus 31:12, 13).

"If you keep your feet from breaking the Sabbath and from doing as you please on my holy day, if you call the Sabbath a delight and the LORD's holy day honorable, and if you honor it by not going your own way and not doing as you please or speaking idle words, then you will find your joy in the LORD, and I will cause you to ride on the heights of the land" (Isaiah 58:13, 14).

"Also I gave them my Sabbaths as a sign between us, so they would know that I the LORD made them holy. . . . Keep my Sabbaths holy, that they may be a sign between us. Then you will know that I am the LORD your God" (Ezekiel 20:12-20).

[17] "There were giants in the earth in those days; and also after that, when the sons of God came in unto the daughters of men, and they bare children to them, the same became mighty men which were of old, men of renown" (Genesis 6:4, KJV).

[18] "After he drove the man out, he placed on the east side of the Garden of Eden cherubim and a flaming sword flashing back and forth to guard the way to the tree of life" (Genesis 3:24).

[19] "Now the LORD God had planted a garden in the east, in Eden; and there he put the man he had formed. And the LORD God made all kinds of trees grow out of the ground—trees that were pleasing to the eye and good for food. In the middle of

the garden were the tree of life and the tree of the knowledge of good and evil."

"The LORD God took the man and put him in the Garden of Eden to work it and take care of it. And the LORD God commanded the man, 'You are free to eat from any tree in the garden; but you must not eat from the tree of the knowledge of good and evil, for when you eat of it you will surely die' " (Genesis 2:8, 9, 15-17).

[20] "Then the man and his wife heard the sound of the LORD God as he was walking in the garden in the cool of the day, and they hid from the LORD God among the trees of the garden" (Genesis 3:8).

[21] "But after he had considered this, an angel of the Lord appeared to him in a dream and said, 'Joseph son of David, do not be afraid to take Mary home as your wife, because what is conceived in her is from the Holy Spirit. She will give birth to a son, and you are to give him the name Jesus, because he will save his people from their sins' " (Matthew 1:20, 21).

"Here is a trustworthy saying that deserves full acceptance: Christ Jesus came into the world to save sinners—of whom I am the worst" (1 Timothy 1:15).

"Since the children have flesh and blood, he too shared in their humanity so that by his death he might destroy him who holds the power of death—that is, the devil—and free those who all their lives were held in slavery by their fear of death. For surely it is not angels he helps, but Abraham's descendants. For this reason he had to be made like his brothers in every way, in order that he might become a merciful and faithful high priest in service to God, and that he might make atonement for the sins of the people. Because he himself suffered when he was tempted, he is able to help those who are being tempted" (Hebrews 2:14-18).

"You see, at just the right time, when we were still powerless, Christ died for the ungodly. Very rarely will anyone die for a righteous man, though for a good man someone might possibly dare to die. But God demonstrates his own love for us in this: While we were still sinners, Christ died for us.

"Since we have now been justified by his blood, how much more shall we be saved from God's wrath through him! For if, when we were God's enemies, we were reconciled to him through the death of his Son, how much more, having been reconciled, shall we be saved through his life! Not only is this so, but we also rejoice in God through our Lord Jesus Christ, through whom we have now received reconciliation" (Romans 5:6-11).

"But he was pierced for our transgressions, he was crushed for our iniquities; the punishment that brought us peace was upon him, and by his wounds we are healed" (Isaiah 53:5).

"The high priest carries the blood of animals into the Most Holy Place as a sin offering, but the bodies are burned outside the camp. And so Jesus also suffered outside the city gate to make the people holy through his own blood" (Hebrews 13:11, 12).

"Just as man is destined to die once, and after that to face judgment, so Christ was sacrificed once to take away the sins of many people; and he will appear a second time, not to bear sin, but to bring salvation to those who are waiting for him" (Hebrews 9:27, 28).

[22] "For the wages of sin is death, but the gift of God is eternal life in Christ Jesus our Lord" (Romans 6:23).

"Therefore, just as sin entered the world through one man, and death through sin, and in this way death came to all men, because all sinned" (Romans 5:12).

[23] "To him who is able to keep you from falling and to present you before his glorious presence without fault and with great joy—to the only God our Savior be glory, majesty, power and authority, through Jesus Christ our Lord, before all ages, now and forevermore! Amen" (Jude 24, 25).

"I will give you a new heart and put a new spirit in you; I will remove from you your heart of stone and give you a heart of flesh. And I will put my Spirit in you and move you to follow my decrees and be careful to keep my laws" (Ezekiel 36:26, 27).

"Through these he has given us his very great and precious promises, so that through them you may participate in the divine nature and escape the corruption in the world caused by evil desires" (2 Peter 1:4).

[24] "To Adam he said, 'Because you listened to your wife and ate from the tree about which I commanded you, "You must not eat of it," Cursed is the ground because of you; through painful toil you will eat of it all the days of your life. It will produce thorns and thistles for you, and you will eat the plants of the field. By the sweat of your brow you will eat your food

until you return to the ground, since from it you were taken; for dust you are and to dust you will return' " (Genesis 3:17-19).

[25] "Adam lay with his wife Eve, and she conceived and gave birth to Cain. She said, 'With the help of the LORD I have brought forth a man.' Later she gave birth to his brother Abel. Now Abel kept flocks, and Cain worked the soil. In the course of time Cain brought some of the fruits of the soil as an offering to the LORD. But Abel brought fat portions from some of the firstborn of his flock. The LORD looked with favor on Abel and his offering, but on Cain and his offering he did not look with favor. So Cain was very angry, and his face was downcast. Then the LORD said to Cain, 'Why are you angry? Why is your face downcast? If you do what is right, will you not be accepted? But if you do not do what is right, sin is crouching at your door; it desires to have you, but you must master it.' Now Cain said to his brother Abel, 'Let's go out to the field.' And while they were in the field, Cain attacked his brother Abel and killed him. Then the LORD said to Cain, 'Where is your brother Abel?'

'I don't know,' he replied. 'Am I my brother's keeper?'

The Lord said, 'What have you done? Listen! Your brother's blood cries out to me from the ground. Now you are under a curse and driven from the ground, which opened its mouth to receive your brother's blood from your hand. When you work the ground, it will no longer yield its crops for you. You will be a restless wanderer on the earth.' Cain said to the LORD, 'My punishment is more than I can bear. Today you are driving me from the land, and I will be hidden from your presence; I will be a restless wanderer on the earth, and whoever finds me will kill me.' But the LORD said to him, 'Not so; if anyone kills Cain, he will suffer vengeance seven times over.' Then the LORD put a mark on Cain so that no one who found him would kill him. So Cain went out from the LORD's presence and lived in the land of Nod, east of Eden" (Genesis 4:1-16).

THE PREACHER

Shaina, deep in thought, dug carefully about the budding daffodils. *How lovely, the soft yellow against gray rock,* she thought. For 12 years she'd nurtured the plants from Eden valley, each time they bloomed renewing her vows of loyalty to the God of Adam. This small cloistered garden had become her retreat when the clamoring world ridiculed her loyalty and nibbled at her simple faith. At first she'd hoped her father would join her in worshiping God each Sabbath, but upon his return from Eden he'd seemed preoccupied, hardly aware of her newfound joy. Ona made no attempt to hide her scorn, and had it not been for Ira the gardener, Shaina's lot would have been a lonely one indeed. But as they worked together in the gardens, she had told him of her grandparents' steady hope and of the experience in Eden valley. Ira confided that he'd always believed, but he knew not how to worship God. Together they prayed and pledged themselves to wait patiently for the Holy One.

But now something had happened that roiled the steady rhythm of Shaina's days. To their door had come a stranger, a cousin from Havilah river land, a rugged man with the tawny grace of her father's people. A maker of musical instruments, he wished to set up a business in the city. Nathan, delighted to have a kinsman in their midst, insisted he stay with them until his business became established. So Ben had become a member of their household, and from the first day, Shaina felt his admiring eyes following her everywhere.

Ira spoke now as he trimmed a small, eager evergreen that clambered profusely over the rock wall. "The young man, he obviously finds you enchanting. What do you think?"

Blushing, Shaina thrust her tool into the soil with more force than necessary. "I'm very inexperienced at this sort of thing. Because they are violent, profane creatures who know nothing of God, I've ignored all the young men Mother brings around. I would rather live alone forever than marry one of them and have to bow down to their ugly gods. But this man from Havilah, surely he worships the true God. He grew up in the fields of Sepp. How could he do otherwise?"

"And do you find him interesting?" the old gardener probed.

"Well," the young woman replied, glancing up shyly from the patch of flowers, "I am obsolutely tongue-tied in his presence, and my heart leaps about in my chest like an acrobat in the marketplace."

Ira chuckled and went about his work, noting that she daydreamed more than she weeded.

That evening, as the family lounged in the ivory room about an open fire that had been built against the chill spring air, Ona spoke from a fur rug she shared with Nathan. "I think we should prepare a feast in Ben's honor, to introduce him to others in the city. His life needs something besides work and these quiet evenings here with us." She smiled at the tall man, who still bore something of his country heritage.

Shaina wondered if he reminded her mother of Nathan when he had arrived in the city long years before, still brown and bearded from the hidden valley of Havilah.

"We'll have feasting and dancing, and this room will be filled with laughter and music, and I will forget that I am no longer a girl." Ona's eyes sparkled in the firelight. "What do you say, Ben? Would it not brighten your life?"

The bearded young man looked up from the instrument he was stringing and laughed, even, white teeth
breaking the golden browns of hair and skin. "You make
it sound very exciting, Ona. But I know nothing of
dancing."

"You drink a little wine and then become as proficient
as the rest," Nathan said wryly. "It is the women, at any
rate, who lend themselves best to the dance."

"I would be honored to meet your friends." Ben pulled
his fingers across the strings, frowning in concentration.
"Shaina, what do you say to all this?"

"She does not like our entertaining," the mother
answered for her daughter. "She thinks we are all a
godless lot."

Ona always left the girl feeling awkward, and tonight
with Ben's eyes upon her, she fumbled for words. "I'm
not sure you'll like the kind of celebrations we have here
in the city, Ben, though my mother has only your
happiness at heart. It is true, I do not enjoy them." Her
sea-green eyes serious and intense, she sat shyly in her
simple linen dress, coppery hair tumbling over her
shoulders.

"But you will come, to please me?" Ben looked at her
with merry, bold eyes, and her heart began that foolish
prancing again.

Scornfully the older woman interrupted once more.
"No, Ben! You'll never entice her, for it will be the
evening and morning of the seventh day, and Shaina
would not set her holy toe into our rowdy midst during
those sacred hours."

Nathan laid his hand upon his wife's arm. "Please,
Ona. Enough. Shaina has a right to her convictions."

"She was fine till you dragged her off to Eden.
Afterward she returned more Abigail's daughter than
mine. And the years have not helped. Show me any other
27-year-old girl who scorns dancing and the company of
young men. Soon I shall betroth her to the son of Zimri,

and she will be forced to take her place within the society of the city and stop this peasant life in the gardens with Ira."

Shaina's heart stood still. She knew well the son of Zimri, a handsome, wealthy scoundrel with cruel eyes.

Nathan spoke, and in his voice was a fury she'd never heard before. "Our daughter will never be betrothed to any man against her wishes, Ona."

Ben rose from his bench and beckoned Shaina to follow. He picked up her long wool wrap and placed it about her shoulders as they entered the gardens. "Sorry I got you into that. Guess there are some pretty strong emotions bottled up in there. I didn't expect to find anyone here in the city who retained the old ways. I remember the time you visited Havilah. I thought you were the most beautiful girl I'd ever seen, and now that you are a woman, you are even lovelier."

"Thank you, Ben. There were so many cousins those brief days at Grandfather's that I had no time to sort you all out, but I love having you here with us. As you can see, my mother is impatient with my beliefs, but I love her deeply, and I know she loves me, too. She does not understand my need to follow Adam's God. What will you do about her plans for sixth night?"

"I shall attend," Ben said quietly.

"Do you not hold sacred the hours of the Sabbath? Have you not seen the lamb burnt upon the altar, and do you not know its holy meaning? Do you not want to greet and commune with God during the special hours He shares with us? Believe me, Ben, Mother's feast will be no place for a follower of the Promised One, on Sabbath eve or any other eve."

"I am tired of those country ways. You were there only briefly. It was a novelty to you, but I want to see how other men live."

"You will see, all right, in this city." Her voice was edgy with her disappointment. "You will see babies offered upon altars while their half-naked mothers leap and dance in the firelight as though their hearts weren't breaking. You will see depravity in all its filthy detail. Men will accost you on the streets and in your place of work, seeking your body for their vile lusts. Your best friend may disappear, never to return, because some thief has hacked him to death and thrown the pieces to the dogs for whatever his purse contained. The day will come, Ben, when you will long to see sheep grazing on the hillsides in your peaceful valley and to hear the voice of Sepp raised in prayer."

Suddenly he turned her toward him in the still, cool night and kissed her gently. "I didn't mean to upset you, Shaina. If you'd been in Havilah, I'd never have left. I know you are right, but I felt confined there, restless to see beyond the hills. Perhaps after your mother's initiation, I shall be content to return. Would you go with me?"

Everything in her longed to say yes to this man she knew so little, but some inner voice urged caution. "I would think about it," she replied, her voice still wobbly from that first unexpected kiss.

On the night of the celebration the house was bright with light, clay lamps burning everywhere, even along the paths throughout the gardens. Nathan's harp and Ben's flute wafted their music out the open windows, and laughter and singing filled the rooms. Standing on the small terrace a few steps beneath her sleeping quarters, Shaina could watch the merrymaking, and her heart ached as she saw Ben, wine cup in hand, boldly appraising the women as their dancing became more suggestive.

This is what he came for, she thought sadly. *Excitement. The tempter Eve met in Eden has a thousand ways to entice men away from God, and Ben is dazzled already.* But what had he said? That after tonight, perhaps he'd return home, and that he would take her with him? She knew she would go. Back to Havilah. To the still nights along the great, shining river and to the safe retreat of Ben's loving care forever. There she would bear children to sit about the tables of Sepp, and never would she be different and lonely again. She decided to go to her own rock-walled garden, away from the raucous laughter and the drunken singing, to pray. But when she was enclosed in its cool, quiet isolation, she could not enter into the still presence of God. Something in her, tightly coiled and expectant, rejected, for the first time, the peace of her beloved spot. Somehow she sensed that what she had there with God might ask a high price of her. She could not pray tonight, but sat, instead, upon a boulder beside the small stream that bubbled over and around rocks. Watching large, drifting clouds fragment into trails of frothy whiteness, she waited, hardly knowing it, for Ben's footstep. When it came, she wasn't terribly surprised.

"I thought I'd find you here." He stood so tall in the moonlight, sturdier, stronger than the city men she knew, dressed in a short belted tunic, leather thongs laced high about his muscular legs. "Come with me to the feast. They are about to start eating. You need not stay long." He hesitated, then approached closer. She could smell the wine upon his breath, and for a fleeting moment thought of how Abigail would mourn his loss of innocence. "I just want them to see how beautiful you are. And that I am not so alone after all."

Her resolve shattered. Alone? Ben, this handsome Havilah man? Was he, indeed, uneasy in the company of Ona's sophisticated friends? His need of her touched her heart as no other argument could have, and she went to his side, indicating her willingness to go. "Only for a short time, Ben. Just until you have met a few people and feel more comfortable. I am not dressed for such an occasion. Are you sure you wish to be seen with me?"

Ben glanced at the pale, green gown draped softly

across one shoulder and knew she would be, in her simplicity, the loveliest woman at the gathering. "You'll do very well," he replied, laughing gently. "You are a true Havilah girl. Beautiful in the best of ways."

She wished he hadn't said that. It reminded her of Abigail, and tonight she didn't want to think of her grandmother. Not on sixth night, when Sepp killed the lamb for all his family's sins.

When they entered the ivory room, all the guests gathered about the long table instantly quieted. They knew Nathan and Ona had a daughter, but they had seen less and less of her in recent years. Now she stood before them on the arm of the young barbarian from Nathan's homeland, and a murmur of delight arose at the sight of the handsome pair. Shaina, glancing at her parents, noted triumph in her mother's eyes and startled sadness in her father's. For the first time she understood how he had sold his soul for Ona. But she would not be so foolish. Tonight she would help Ben find acceptance among the crafty city dwellers, and by tomorrow he would have seen enough, and would ask her parents if he could take her back to Havilah. Her mother would be difficult, but her father would rejoice, and in the end, enable her to go.

The next day, however, produced no such miracle. Ben thought the ongoing feast a huge success. Ona kept the tables piled high with delicacies. Nathan entered into the festivities only as much as courtesy demanded, and Shaina slipped away to her bed soon after the midnight feasting ended.

When, on the morning of first day, the last guests straggled homeward, Nathan surveyed the debris skeptically. "Are you sure, Ona, that it's worth it?"

His wife laid wearily upon a couch, dark circles beneath her eyes. "Oh, Nathan, you are always so grim. There are servants to put the house back in order. And the guests will long remember this celebration for your kinsman. You will be labeled a generous host with a beautiful wife and daughter. What more could you ask?"

"A garden whose every nook has not been soiled with the evils of humanity. And a daughter who retains her simple love for God."

"What are you talking about? Shaina stayed but a few hours sixth night, and that only to please Ben, I'm sure. At any rate, it's time she took her place within society. I heard many compliments among the guests about her beauty. With a few jewels and some experience with cosmetics, she could have her pick of the young men, I expect. Aren't you proud of her, Nathan?"

"I'm proud of her loyalty to God, Ona. I don't want it compromised, ever."

"You are unrealistic, my love. She cannot live out her days with no more than old Ira for a friend and a walled garden for a lover. Can't you see her joy in Ben? He is, perhaps, your God's answer to her loneliness. After all, he was raised in Havilah, is used to their ways of worship, and would tolerate Shaina's peculiarities."

"Her peculiarities?" His voice rose dangerously. "Tolerate them? Ona, I do not want a man for Shaina who *tolerates* her purity. I want one who *values* it. Ben is not the one. In His time God will provide, if Shaina can be patient."

Ona laid her hand on her husband's arm. "Be calm, Nathan," she said quietly. "You are reacting out of your own sorrow over having married me, and cruelty ill becomes you. Perhaps in the end Shaina will prove wiser than her father, and Ben will have to look elsewhere. But yes or no, you cannot force her decision. Your God is a god of freedom—you told me so yourself. That's why He allowed Eve to eat the fruit. You must give Shaina the same liberty, my darling."

He sat on the floor beside her couch and rested his head in her lap. She stroked his hair, and they did not speak. Each knew the other's thoughts well.

* * * * *

The weeks and months that followed were for Shaina sometimes ecstatically happy, at other times fraught with a gnawing fear. She felt herself slipping away from God in spite of the hours she spent in her garden seeking Him. Ira watched her struggle with deep concern, praying devoutly for her.

Shaina loved to walk in the marketplace with Ben. The inhabitants of the city had a curious respect for him—for his size and his strength, but something more beside. A latent power, which attracted women and placed upon men a cautious restraint. There was a boldness about him that opened doors and also a gentleness bred into his very being from a long line of God-fearing ancestors. When she was with him, Shaina felt that nothing mattered but to walk by his side, know his love, and make him glad. But other times, when she knelt alone in her garden, she knew Ben was slowly, imperceptibly coming between her and God. The dream of a return to Havilah soon died. Ben's business thrived, and he talked of building a home for them, a home where she could create the loveliest gardens in the city. Everyone simply assumed they would marry. It became more and more difficult to set seventh day apart as sacred time, so easy to live like the rest. To give up her lonely vigil. Sometimes she heard Adam's voice: "Are you brave, child, brave enough?" But she pushed the memory from her and thought of Ben, golden Ben, whose laughter made all serious matters seem ridiculously somber.

One windy, sun-spattered day Shaina and Ben rode down into the city from an afternoon of exploring in the surrounding hills. Windblown and ruddy with color, they made a stunning sight upon their handsome steeds as they picked their way among the pedestrians along the dusty thoroughfare. They soon noted a large crowd gathered in the open area about a community well, and beckoning her to follow, Ben urged his horse toward the fringes of the group. From their elevated position, they could see a man at the center, standing upon the base of the well and speaking to the people thronging about him. Some listened intently, others walked away guffawing or muttering oaths. In spite of the rabble, it wasn't difficult to hear. His voice, powerful and penetrating, fell upon her ears as if they were alone upon the street, for he spoke of God—not idly or speculatively, but as one who knew Him. He talked of judgment, and an authority in his voice left no serious listener without a holy fear. Shaina understood those who eased away with nervous banter. She longed to join them, to put space between herself and this stranger, to ride beside Ben in the sunshine and live only for today, this easy, joyous day.

But something about the man held her: a radiance in his face, an undercurrent of deep, loving concern that stirred old loyalties within her.

"Who is he?" Ben inquired of someone standing nearby.

"Called Enoch by name," [1] the man replied. "He's passed through here once or twice before. Usually takes a convert or two back to the hills with him if he doesn't get chased out of the city too soon. Don't know why I listen. Gives me nightmares for a week afterward. You'd think he knew the Almighty to hear him, and by the look of his face, he well may."

"Let's get out of here," Ben muttered.

"No, Ben. I must hear this man out. Every word."

Ben knew that Shaina, usually so compliant, was not going to budge, and recognizing also that it was far too dangerous to leave her alone, he prepared, with a sigh of resignation, to wait.

Enoch spoke more softly now. His listeners had thinned to 15 or 20. Shaina noted Ira among their number and smiled at him fondly.

"I have spoken of judgment, of God's plan to destroy

this wretched, unbelieving generation, but friends, this is a strange, sad work for our Creator. He who put our first parents in Eden loves us still. His few demands are for our safety and happiness.[2] He asks only that we trust and obey Him, accepting His love, a love so great He will sacrifice the Promised One to reinstate us once more into His divine family. Friends," his voice reached into each heart with an almost tangible intensity of pleading, "come out of this city. Come to the mountains, where we worship in simplicity, making Him first in everything. Look about you. There is murder and theft, drunkenness, false worship, and every perversion of man's sexual powers. Your lives are ever in danger, and even if you are rich and powerful, your *soul* is in danger. *Think,* my brothers and sisters. *Think.* Do not be lulled into eternal loss. In the morning I leave this place. Those of you who wish to dedicate yourself to the true and living God, meet me here at daybreak, and we will travel together to a place where the voice of prayer and praise rises every morning to Him who loves us and will redeem us." The man stepped from the platform and disappeared down a side street.

Without a word, Shaina reined her horse about and headed homeward. Ben, still beside her, spoke at last, uneasily. "He disturbed you. I wish we had not stopped."

"That's the problem, Ben. We all wish not to be disturbed. Instead we want to live out our lives in feasting and idleness, hoping the ugliness of this rebellious world will never touch us. Ignoring death, pretending it will never happen, or that if it does, the great, kind merciful God will overlook our years of defiance and whisk us off to some magical land where we can go right on in our wicked ways. Did not this man's words fall upon your heart like a sword, Ben?"

"Actually, they were a bit like the lecture Abigail gave me before I left home," he admitted ruefully. "I've been relieved not to hear that sort of thing for a while."

"Remember what he said, Ben? *Think.* Instead of running away from reality, that's what we should do. *Think.* Oh, my beloved, we are heading down a long, wrong road."

They rode up the tree-lined entrance toward Nathan's home in silence. Enoch's words had left her shaken. She saw clearly, as if God Himself had spoken to her, that in marrying Ben she would cut herself off from the God of the universe.

That night at the table she told of the afternoon's experience.

"What did he look like, this preacher of doom?" Ona asked, coiling one long lock of dark hair idly about her finger.

Shaina thought a moment and shrugged. "I can't honestly say, Mother. I guess I wasn't really seeing him, only listening."

"His face shone in a supernatural way." Ben struggled to reconstruct the scene. "And what he said was truth. I believe the most evil man in the crowd recognized it as truth. The message of this man Enoch bore some kind of holy seal. I would prefer not to have heard it."

"Oh, Ben, do not take it all so seriously," Ona told him. "These fanatics who stand on street corners and rant about the God of Adam are just disturbed individuals who do not know how to enjoy the bounties of the earth and don't want anyone else to, either. Come, eat and relax, and let us speak of the house you and Shaina will build. Nathan told me only this morning he will send Ira with you when you marry to help Shaina in her plans to beautify the place. She is very clever, this daughter of mine, and you will have a place to turn the head of every passerby." Ona poured a cup of wine and set it before Ben, patting his head in a soothing gesture.

"Will he speak again tomorrow?" Nathan inquired. "I regret I did not hear him."

His wife sighed. "You are all alike. The blood of Abigail runs thick in your veins, and you can never be free of your obsession with that God of yours. You have my sympathy."

"You should count your blessings, Mother," Shaina teased. "Father is one of the few men in the city with only one wife.[3] Surely, you can thank the blood of Abigail and the fear of God for that. Is it not something for which to be grateful?"

Ona smiled, that sultry, full-lipped smile that had beguiled Nathan long years before. "That thought has crossed my mind, darling."

Nathan turned toward his daughter. "There is no other who even tempts me, Shaina. I would like to believe it is great virtue on my part, but the truth of the matter is that I love your mother beyond all reason. Look at her. Where else could one find such beauty?"

"Only in her daughter," Ben countered loyally. "And I agree, Nathan. I too could never love another."

Ona, pleased at her husband's declaration, said to her daughter, "Whether you know it or not, such loyalty is bred into your very bones. It's part of your heritage. That much, Shaina, we do indeed owe to Abigail."

"To answer your question, Father, Enoch will leave in the morning for his mountain retreat. He has invited anyone who wants to come with him."

"You'd better stand guard over her tonight, Ben," Ona warned. "Shaina has a tendency to take this sort of thing very seriously." Her manner was light, but they all heard the apprehension in her voice.

"Never fear, Mother. Father once said he was a coward most of the time, and I guess I'm not unlike him." Instantly she knew she had pierced her father's heart, and she berated herself both for her unintended cruelty and their mutual weakness.

---

[1] "Enoch, the seventh from Adam, prophesied about these

men: 'See, the Lord is coming with thousands upon thousands of his holy ones to judge everyone, and to convict all the ungodly of all the ungodly acts they have done in the ungodly way, and of all the harsh words ungodly sinners have spoken against him' " (Jude 14, 15).

"When Jared had lived 162 years, he became the father of Enoch. And after he became the father of Enoch, Jared lived 800 years and had other sons and daughters. Altogether, Jared lived 962 years, and then he died.

"When Enoch had lived 65 years, he became the father of Methuselah. And after he became the father of Methuselah, Enoch walked with God 300 years and had other sons and daughters. Altogether, Enoch lived 365 years. Enoch walked with God; then he was no more, because God took him away" (Genesis 5:18-24).

[2] "The LORD commanded us to obey all these decrees and to fear the LORD our God, so that we might always prosper and be kept alive" (Deuteronomy 6:24).

"See, I set before you today life and prosperity, death and destruction. For I command you today to love the LORD your God, to walk in his ways, and to keep his commands, decrees and laws; then you will live and increase, and the LORD your God will bless you in the land you are entering to possess" (Deuteronomy 30:15, 16).

"To do your will, O my God, is my desire; your law is within my heart" (Psalm 40:8).

"Now all has been heard; here is the conclusion of the matter: Fear God and keep his commandments, for this is the whole duty of man. For God will bring every deed into judgment, including every hidden thing, whether it is good or evil" (Ecclesiastes 12:13, 14).

"Obey me, and I will be your God and you will be my people. Walk in all the ways I command you, that it may go well with you" (Jeremiah 7:23).

[3] "Lamech married two women, one named Adah and the other Zillah" (Genesis 4:19).

THE DECISION

A year had passed since Enoch's powerful message had momentarily rippled the peace of the city. On a slight elevation, near the western walls, a beautiful edifice of finest cedar took shape in preparation for Ben and Shaina's marriage. Each day Shaina and Ira strolled about the shaded property planning the landscaping, having foraged far afield to find the most rare and exotic plants. For they saw it all in their mind's eye, those two, the sloping expanse of green interspersed with graceful trees, rock walls and shrubbery, water in fountains and streams piped in from the surrounding hills, and color everywhere. Sometimes as they worked, Ira spoke soberly to Shaina of her diminishing faith, and the pain of loss would be strong within her, but it took only a glimpse of Ben to erase such thoughts from her mind. He loved her with an exuberant obsession that she could not resist. If he came more and more to enjoy the life of the city, she chose not to notice. When the house was complete, they would wed, and Ona was already planning a week of festivities such as her friends had never seen. She would present her daughter in the richest materials the passing caravans had to offer, and the legend of her beauty would travel afar. Nathan would be proud and forget his foolish longings for his peasant roots. He would see, at last, that she had planned well for Shaina, that she had been a good mother after all.

They sat one evening, the four of them, relaxing over what Ben called their Havilah meal of simple breads and fruits, when a servant entered to announce a visitor who did not wait to be summoned, but followed close upon the man's heels. Nathan leaped up in astonishment.

"Adriel! What are you doing here?" He encircled him in a great hug. Shaina recognized the man as one of her father's younger brothers, and she had a chilling premonition that he was the bearer of bad tidings.

After the emotional reunion and an introduction to Ona, Adriel seated himself at the table but refused the food urged upon him. Before he could speak, Nathan noted his pale and haggard features. "You look exhausted, my brother. You need rest. Come, I will arrange for you to bathe and sleep. We can talk later."

Shaina thought how much alike they all looked, the Havilah men. Only her father was of slighter build, a more aesthetic man. She loved Ben's strength. He reminded her of the lion they had seen by the lake, with his coiled, sinewy magnetism.

Adriel broke into her reverie with words that startled them all into horrified silence. "I cannot sleep, Nathan. I come bearing the most terrible of messages. The family, the people of Havilah, they are all dead. Our home is destroyed. The valley is lost to us."

"What are you saying, Adriel?" Ben demanded. "Have you gone mad?"

"No, Ben, I am quite sane. A tribe from the north, the people of Yadin, have taken our land and our children and killed the adults." His voice broke, and he could not go on. Nathan, seated beside him, placed an arm about his shoulders and wept with him. Shaina searched Ben's face, but found it set in detached, controlled lines.

When he could speak once more, Adriel resumed his story. "I had been weeks with the sheep in an upper meadow, several miles from the main camp. Each sixth day, young Dur, son of Elrad, brought me food and spent the Sabbath with me. When he did not come one week, I thought only that they needed him in the camp. I had enough supplies by supplementing them with wild berries and fruit. But when he did not arrive the follow-ing week, I feared some beast had harmed him along the way. I decided I must leave the sheep and search for him, so I drove the flock into a gorge and blocked the entrance with boulders for their safety. Then I set out to look for him. As I rode up the valley I noted a strange silence in the fields—no hymns of praise rising, no sign of our kinsmen working. Just an ominous quiet every-where. I rode up onto the hillside and made my way cautiously through the trees, being careful to stay out of sight. You know, Nathan, where the river makes a sharp bend and the camp lies just beyond? Well, at that point I saw a sight that struck terror to my heart, for armed guards rode the circuit of the camp and hundreds, maybe thousands, were building—*building*, Nathan—in our valley. They are creating a city.

"And in Mother's gardens, the beautiful rock gardens she had built on the hillside in honor of Yahweh, they were making a grove. A great golden image stood in the middle of Mother's creation, and the poppies sprang crimson among the rocks like tears of blood at the sacrilege." Adriel bowed his head sobbing, and Shaina felt tears upon her own cheeks.

It was Ona who spoke at last. "This is a terrible tale, Adriel. Can you go on?" Shaina reached out to take Ben's hand as her uncle continued. Nathan sat pale as death.

"There were young children, our children, working as slaves in the fields close to home, but not a grown Havilah man or woman; only a smoking heap, where their bodies had been burned far down the valley."

"The servants? They did not spare the servants?" Ben asked.

Adriel laughed bitterly. "The invaders well knew the servants would rise up against them when the opportu-nity arose. They were followers of the true God, every one, and a loved segment of our father's family, treated as sons and daughters. However much the enemy may have wanted their services, they knew better than to spare them."

Shaina tried to imagine the valley bereft of Sepp and his holy altar—of Abigail, bronzed and smiling in the joy of her sacred hope. Well, they would sleep with Adam until the Promised One made all things right. She wondered how. Abigail and Adam had spoken of the coming One and His death. But what then? What of those who had returned to the dust? Would they live again?

"There was nothing I could do." Adriel forced himself to finish the story. "Not even for the children." Shaina felt his agony deep in her soul. "I decided to come and tell you and Ben, lest you make a trip for clay, Nathan, and stumble upon the nightmare."

Shaina heard her mother suck in her breath sharply. "What will you do without clay, Nathan?"

Her husband stared at her in angry astonishment. "At a time like this you think of clay, Ona? My parents are dead. My brothers are dead. My people are gone. And you think of clay?"

She faced him coolly. "It is our livelihood, Nathan. And there is nothing we can do for the dead."

"I expect he can acquire the clay for a price. He is not, after all, a follower of God, and they will count him as one of their own." As his brother's words burned into him Nathan's eyes registered a pain from which Shaina turned away.

Late that night, when all had retired to their sleeping quarters, Shaina slipped out to her garden. It had been a long time since she had gone there, her interests having shifted to the landscaping of her new home. The garden looked just as it had before, and she knew that Ira's loving hands had kept it that way. Suddenly there in the darkness she cried terrible racking sobs for the grandmother she would never see again, for the valley that had been her spiritual home. Was her father, too, weeping, or must he stifle his mourning before the woman who could never understand? Must the tears linger forever unshed in his heart? All at once she realized that she had saved her own tears for this place. She had not gone to the comfort of Ben's arms, sensing that he, too, would not understand. Havilah valley had been his childhood home far more than hers. The smoke of his parents' dying had drifted over the shining river of his boyhood. Yet this night he had left the room without a word or a tear, as though irritated by the break in their routine. Asking no question about his younger brothers and sisters, he had rejected his roots in a way never possible for Nathan.

His reaction left her troubled. Did she really know this man soon to become her husband? She had loved his smile, his body, his joy, his adoration of her, and had been satisfied with that. What lay beneath the exterior?

Who would guard the faith of Sepp and Abigail? Only Adriel survived, and where would he find another godly wife? As she thought of him now lying beneath the soft wool coverlets of her mother's guest quarters, she tried to imagine his sorrow as he mourned his wife and his 13-year-old daughter.

Impulsively, she decided to go to him. "Adriel, my kinsman," she whispered at his open window, "it is Shaina. May I come in?"

He bade her enter and she saw him in the dim light of his clay lamp, sitting up in bed, his eyes red, his face swollen. She went and sat beside him, taking his large calloused hand in hers.

"I have come to grieve with you, Adriel. To carry a little of your sorrow. I loved them too, especially my grandmother." They sat quietly together, weeping in the gentle darkness, and later she went her way without a word.

Nathan did not go to his workshop for days, saying he had no heart for it. Both he and Adriel picked at their food and grew thin. Ona scolded and cajoled to no avail.

"Really, Father, you two must eat," Shaina urged one sunny morning as she plied them with melons and bowls of steaming barley glistening with honey.

Cutting the cool fruit listlessly, her father smiled sadly. "It's odd. I went home only twice a year. I saw them so little. Yet thinking of Havilah without my mother there, without her smile and her greeting, leaves me ill. I cannot think of food. It turns my stomach. And Adriel's grief is worse. The blood of his wife and child lies fresh upon that loved soil. Can you really expect us to eat?"

Ben, seated on his right, ate with relish. "Nothing will bring back Havilah or our family. Grandfather Sepp feared this invasion. He spoke often to us of its possibility. And he told us not to fight. He wanted no bloodshed. He said the land and our lives were not important—only obedience to God. It was one reason I left. I had no desire to find myself trapped in that valley, the victim of any foe who came along."

"Even if we *had* fought, Ben, we'd have been no match for their numbers and their weaponry. And Father was right. Warfare is of the evil one. It is better to die at peace with God than to slash and kill for a few more years of life."

"That's easy for you to say," the younger man replied testily. "You are alive and well. Do you think those who lie in the smoking heap would agree?"

Adriel looked his cocky young nephew squarely in the eye. "I wish to God I had died with them, for my life without them is bitter. But you know nothing of such sorrow. The Lord forgive you for your foolish words and your disloyalty to Him and to your family."

Rising from his chair abruptly, controlling his anger, Ben left for his place of business.

"Please excuse him, Adriel," Shaina urged gently. "He seems edgy lately. Not himself."

"He resents me here," the refugee said, not unkindly.

"I remind him of all he hoped to leave behind. My grief annoys him. It is time for me to go, Nathan. I have been meaning to discuss my plans with you, and now is as good a time as any. You must return to your clay, and I must take up my life once more. Our mother would have little patience with our indolence and our tears."

Shaina laughed in relief at his words. "You are right, Adriel. She would say, 'I'm ashamed of you two. Put your trust in the Promised One and live responsibly upon the earth. Stop mourning for us. We sleep in faith.' " [1]

"You sound just like her, child." Nathan glanced at his daughter fondly. "So what are your plans, brother? I wish you would stay safely here with us."

"I cannot, though I'm loath to leave you. But—forgive me—I cannot stay in this house where idols stare at me from every corner and no one worships God. Nathan, you have been kind, and Ona has been gracious and understanding. You have given me time to mourn.

"I have thought much about the future. The prophet Enoch—surely you have heard of him—predicts a judgment to come upon the earth that will destroy all mankind except those committed to Him. [2] I dare not live in this city, Nathan. I see what has happened to you and to Ben. So subtly evil invades the life, and I am no less susceptible than you, my brother. I must go where God is worshiped and where all nature speaks of Him daily in sunsets and mountains and lakes. Enoch taught Father how to find his valley, and Father in turn taught each of us, his sons. Just for a time like this. Next first day I shall set out to find the place, for it is one of the few spots left where God's people worship Him in peace and safety. It is a far journey, but I am eager to be on my way."

"You cannot go alone, Adriel." Nathan's voice was tight with concern.

"He will not have to, Father," Shaina said quietly. "I will accompany him. And Ira, too, wishes to go. He has longed to since Enoch spoke here in the city, but he was reluctant to ask for his release."

"Shaina, you do not understand. Adriel will not be returning. He speaks of making his home there."

"I understand fully, Father. I too speak of making my home there."

"But what of Ben? Your marriage? Your new home? Your mother? Shaina, we must talk about this. You're acting upon impulse."

She heard the fear in his voice and steeled herself against it. "Father, I am nearly 30. This is no childish whim." Seeing her mother standing in the doorway, she wondered how long she had been listening. "I have known almost from the start that I would have to choose between Ben and God. Ben has hardened his heart against the teachings of his childhood. That is why he cannot mourn his family. When he rode away, he had to destroy, within his mind, Havilah and all it contained. He soon saw that to be popular and successful here, he must dismiss God as well. He felt that in time I would do the same. Adriel is right. This world is in increasing rebellion against God. One must walk away from sin or be engulfed by it. At first, when Ben fell in love with me, I convinced myself that I could have him and God, too. Soon, however, I saw his slow disintegration and felt myself slipping downward with him, but I no longer cared. I wanted him too much. He was Havilah to me, and I loved Havilah.

"When Enoch spoke, it stirred my heart. Since then it has been harder to still my conscience, but I had not the courage to leave Ben. I truly love him." Her voice trembled, but she went on. "Now Havilah is gone. I realize it was not the place I longed for, but the love of God I felt there. It was in the people, and it lives on in Adriel and Ira and Enoch and God's followers everywhere, however few. But not in Ben."

"Nor in us," her mother said bitterly, tears streaming down her cheeks.

Half-crazed with the thought of losing her, Nathan exploded, "Shaina, I forbid you to go."

Ona quickly slipped to his side, holding his head against her, stroking his hair. "Nathan, my darling, remember she is free. Free to choose God or this hunk of silver." She nudged a nearby image with her toe. "It was you who took her to Abigail and then to Eden. You have led her to this moment. Do not make it hard for her." And they clung to each other, pale and still.

Shaina sought Adriel's eyes for strength and found it. He understood her decision and what it cost her, and as she passed him to console her sorrowing parents, he lightly touched her shoulder.

That night she asked Ben to walk with her in the gardens, and there, with her heart thumping wildly and fighting for control of her emotions, she told him of her decision to leave with Adriel.

Ben remained silent until she finished, and then he seized her roughly by the shoulders. "Shaina, don't leave me," he said brokenly. "There is nothing here in this place for me with you gone. I cannot ever love the superficial women of this city. I've still too much of the valley in me. I'll never love anyone but you. I promise you I'll bring no images into the house. You can worship your God—or no one at all. Just don't leave me."

"Why don't you come with us to Enoch's valley?" She willed him to say yes.

"I can't. Long ago I came to hate the worship of God and all its restrictions. Even for you, I cannot go." He turned away from Shaina and nervously clenched and unclenched his fist. "I want power. That's why I like it here. These people respect power. We understand each other."

"Adam said that is what the evil one wanted—power.[3] It is a dangerous desire, Ben. Better to leave the power to God." She did not urge him further. His admission had shown her he would bring only dissension to Enoch's valley.

"Why did Adriel have to come here? We soon would have married and moved into our home. You were happy enough before."

"We would have known the same terrible sorrows my parents have suffered. Deep down, I knew it all along, but I loved you so much I would not allow myself to think of it. And surely, Ben, you knew it too."

He held her in his arms, and as her tears stained his tunic, Shaina felt her girlhood and her happiness slipping away. Adriel could never again say Ben knew nothing of sorrow, for the sounds of his anguish tore harshly into the soft summer night.

* * * * *

The moment of departure had arrived, and Shaina steadied herself against the waves of terror and sadness that washed over her. What was she doing, heading into the wilderness with Ira and Adriel? Where was she going? Would she ever see the faces of her parents again? Who *was* this God who asked such a thing of her? Could He never speak directly to her—never show His face? Yet, deep within something sang sweet and clear, a thin, sure blessing on her journey. She held onto it tenaciously when her father's agonized face ripped into her resolution.

Ben had immediately moved into their partially completed home, so she had not seen him since the night in the garden. It startled her now as he appeared in the dim, early morning light.

Adriel headed toward him, reaching out in a welcoming gesture. "Ben, I'm glad you came. I want to speak to you. We are sons of Sepp, men of Havilah. Come with us. You are a proud, restless man, hungry for authority. Do not be angry," he said, noting the other's sudden glowering. "I recognize these traits in you because I was much like you at the same age. Abigail would tell you I was the most headstrong of her sons. She trembled for me, and rightly so.

"Once we were watching the sheep, Mother and I, and I chafed under those simple pastoral duties. She said to me, 'Adriel, you are like a young lion stalking the earth, hungry for adventure, seeking something over which to exercise control. But, my son, *there is no power worth coveting except the power over one's weaknesses, and only Yahweh can bestow that.*' [4]

" 'I cannot help how I feel,' I told her sullenly.

" 'But God can change all that,' she said. 'You must pray.'

"I told her I did not even like to pray.

"She said, 'Kneel, Adriel.' I can see her yet, holding a black lamb in her arms, all golden against that great, blue bowl of sky over Havilah. And because I adored her, I knelt.

" 'You only have to say four words, Adriel. Just four words: "Lord, make me humble." Say them, son.'

"So, kneeling there in the grasses of the upper meadow, feeling foolish, I prayed the four words. She put her hands on my shoulders and looked at me fiercely. 'Now, keep on praying them every day. The Lord's work in you will not be easy.'

"For some unexplainable reason I did continue saying that simple prayer, almost in defiance. To prove it couldn't be done, this character reversal she predicted.

"But Ben, the ways of God are past understanding. Slowly, I felt myself changing. I wasn't so eager to fight, to elbow my way to the forefront. And I began to know the truth of my mother's words, that power over our weaknesses was all we'd have time for in this world. I began to plead for that power. I didn't mind watching the sheep anymore, for there in that beautiful meadow I learned to talk with God and to experience a happiness I'd never believed possible.

"Come with us, Ben, and learn to pray my mother's prayer." Shaina thought no one could resist the tender pleading in Adriel's voice. She saw the struggle in Ben's face, and every fiber of her being cried out to him to yield, but in the end he turned and disappeared into the darkness without a word.

Nathan and Ona, deeply moved by Adriel's words, stood quiet and resigned as Shaina embraced them, then mounted Hadesh. She glanced back just once as they slipped out onto the street, and saw the home and gardens she had so loved outlined sharply against the first soft pinks of dawn. Her mother raised an arm in farewell, and Shaina locked the picture into her mind for all time.

[1] "Brothers, we do not want you to be ignorant about those who fall asleep, or to grieve like the rest of men, who have no hope" (1 Thessalonians 4:13).

"After he had said this, he went on to tell them, 'Our friend Lazarus has fallen asleep; but I am going there to wake him up.' His disciples replied, 'Lord, if he sleeps, he will get better.' Jesus had been speaking of his death, but his disciples thought he meant natural sleep. So then he told them plainly, 'Lazarus is dead' " (John 11:11-14).

"Then he fell on his knees and cried out, 'Lord, do not hold this sin against them.' When he had said this, he fell asleep" (Acts 7:60).

"Then those also who have fallen asleep in Christ are lost. . . . But Christ has indeed been raised from the dead, the firstfruits of those who have fallen asleep" (1 Corinthians 15:18, 20).

"Multitudes who sleep in the dust of the earth will awake: some to everlasting life, others to shame and everlasting contempt" (Daniel 12:2).

[2] "Enoch, the seventh from Adam, prophesied about these men: 'See, the Lord is coming with thousands upon thousands of his holy ones to judge everyone, and to convict all the ungodly of all the ungodly acts they have done in the ungodly way, and of all the harsh words ungodly sinners have spoken against him' " (Jude 14, 15).

³ "You said in your heart, 'I will ascend to heaven; I will raise my throne above the stars of God; I will sit enthroned on the mount of assembly, on the utmost heights of the sacred mountain. I will ascend above the tops of the clouds; I will make myself like the Most High' " (Isaiah 14:13, 14).

"Through your widespread trade you were filled with violence, and you sinned. So I drove you in disgrace from the mount of God, and I expelled you, O guardian cherub, from among the fiery stones" (Ezekiel 28:16).

⁴ "Do not be overcome by evil, but overcome evil with good" (Romans 12:21).

"He who overcomes will inherit all this, and I will be his God and he will be my son" (Revelation 21:7).

"For everyone born of God overcomes the world. This is the victory that has overcome the world, even our faith" (1 John 5:4).

"Therefore, if anyone is in Christ, he is a new creation; the old has gone, the new has come" (2 Corinthians 5:17).

"Create in me a pure heart, O God, and renew a steadfast spirit within me. Do not cast me from your presence or take your Holy Spirit from me. Restore to me the joy of your salvation and grant me a willing spirit, to sustain me. Then I will teach transgressors your ways, and sinners will turn back to you" (Psalm 51:10-13).

THE VALLEY

The first days of travel were wearying for both Ira and Shaina. His 600 years had slowed his pace a bit, though daily work in the gardens had kept him fit. Shaina's life had been easy—too easy—yet she was an excellent horsewoman, and she surprised Adriel with her endurance. He set a fast pace, pushing relentlessly through the forest with only brief breaks for rest and food. They seldom conversed, each lost in his own grief. Ira unobtrusively tended Shaina's needs until she at last gravely protested, "Ira, you are no longer a servant. My father declared your freedom. We are friends, that is all."

"It is as a daughter I care for you," he replied, smiling. "I have no other kin."

She hugged him impulsively. "And you are my spiritual father. We will care for each other."

"And who will care for me?" Adriel asked, a hint of mischief flickering momentarily in his sad eyes.

"We both will!" Ira and Shaina shouted in unison, their voices echoing strangely in the vast, quiet forest. And they laughed, all at once. For the first time. They were bonded, the three of them, there where the mighty trees shut out all but thin fingers of sunlight which caressed, now and then, the clear colors of brilliant minerals and gemstones scattered upon the forest floor.

One night, while Ira and Adriel sat before the fire discussing the direction of the next day's travel and Shaina prepared for sleep in her small tent, she felt something hard in the bottom of the leather pouch that contained her supply of grooming aids. Pulling it out, she held it curiously in the faint firelight coming through the tent opening, and recognized it at once. It was a blue clay comb, one her father had made her mother years before. Ona had worn it on only the most special of occasions. A delicate spray of flowers was all that showed once the comb was inserted—roses, daisies, tiny leaves, and a little vine that hung fragile and exquisite from the spray of flowers. The three daisies were centered with minute diamonds, which twinkled now in the firelight.

She remembered all the times as a little girl when she'd begged to wear it and her mother had tucked it into her hair, cautioning her not to swing her head about, and leaving it in only for the briefest moments. She'd understood, in those far-off days, that it symbolized the bittersweet love between her parents, and she had valued the trinket as highly as did her mother.

Now, holding it here in the firelight, she knew a terrible longing for those two who had given her life. She ran her fingers over the smooth finish, imagining her father's sandy head bent above the demanding task, thinking only of Ona's joy in the gift. And with a rush of tears she saw her mother tucking the treasure into her daughter's pouch, pouring out the best she had, that Shaina might know, some lonely night far from home, the measure of her love. Wrapping it carefully in the softest of her undergarments, she went to sleep holding it in her hand, strangely comforted.

Each morning they ate boiled grain that had steamed all night over the coals of the fire, knelt upon the moist, aromatic floor of the forest to pray, and then continued, trusting God and the map in Adriel's mind. They forded great rivers, rode days through forests so deep and dark that they fell into grim, depressed silence, only to have the wilderness break at last into a mountain meadow filled with sunlight and flowers and animals so tame they frolicked about the travelers like lambs.

"This must have been how it was in Eden," Shaina said reverently as they lifted the burdens from the horses and freed them to graze.

When she had laid out some of the hard breads and the last of the raisins, Ira returned with a huge cupped leaf overflowing with crimson berries.

"Well, a feast, indeed," Adriel smiled as he cracked pecans big as hen's eggs and laid the tender meats alongside the raisins. "And how appropriate, for I have a splendid announcement which calls for just such a celebration. As I followed this wild river upstream searching for food I found that just beyond the bend this meadow leads into another in which lies the entrance to Enoch's valley. As you can see, there is no hint of it from here. One could travel through and never dream of its existence. If my calculations are correct, we have arrived. So let us rest and eat well. We will bathe and wash our travel-stained garments and present ourselves tomorrow to the holy citizens of Enoch's valley."

"I am a bit afraid," Shaina admitted, reluctantly. "Perhaps I am not holy enough."

"Nor I," Adriel said quietly. "Let us pray we will bring no discord to this place that is a haven for the sons of God."

The three of them knelt in the flower-strewn grass, thanked God for their safe journey, and asked for spiritual cleansing as they joined with Enoch and his converts. Around them a flock of birds, brilliant as gems, sang melodies that seemed to Shaina almost human in their precise, sweet clarity.

Next morning they made their way gently upward through the bright meadow in which they had slept, following along the river into yet another field of grass, flowers, and grazing deer. Ira and Shaina, expecting to find the valley of which Adriel had spoken, looked at their leader questioningly.

Adriel smiled at their confusion. "Enoch planned wisely and well, my friends. Father told us when we rode out of the forest into two meadows, connected by a bend in an untamed torrent of a river, that we had arrived. He said that in the second meadow, which would offer no obvious clue, there would be a wild grapevine growing upon a bitter cherry tree. At that point one must push his way through a stand of brush and then through a narrow opening in a cliff. Yesterday I found the bitter cherry with the vine and the slot in the rock, but went no further, wishing to share the moment of discovery with you who have borne with me the hardships of travel." He hesitated. "I also needed the comfort of your presence. I hope we will find a welcome."

They rode wordlessly past the gnarled tree with its profusion of vines hiding any sign of a path. Adriel dismounted and pulled aside an opening in the underbrush through which Shaina and Ira rode carefully, making every effort to leave no sign of their passing. A bit to their left, in a rocky cliff, appeared an opening so narrow that Shaina had to speak sharply to urge Hadesh through. Once on the other side, the three found themselves gazing at a place of incredible beauty. It wasn't like either Havilah or Eden, Shaina thought, remembering their sprawling and fertile expanse. An enclosed paradise, it was a small world of its own. The few dwellings that dotted the encircling hillsides blended so perfectly into their settings that one had to look carefully to be sure of their presence at all. Water leaped and foamed down a mountainside, shattering sunlight as it broke over rock and stone, to flow, at last, peacefully into a tiny lake shining from the valley floor. Crops and gardens grew in little terraces upon the hillsides, and horses, cattle, and sheep grazed peacefully in the morning sun.

"You did well, Adriel. I often wondered if we could

possibly find such a remote spot." Admiration warmed Ira's voice as he placed his hand upon the younger man's shoulder.

"Surely God was our guide," Adriel responded.

They rode hesitantly toward a weathered structure larger than the others, situated on a slight knoll, assuming it to be the dwelling of Enoch. A tall, dark-haired woman drew back, startled, at their appearance in her dooryard where she ground grain upon a round, hollowed stone.

"We are followers of the true God. Fear not," Adriel said quickly, gently, noting the fear in her soft brown eyes.

She stepped forward, then smiling, said, "I am Rimona, wife of Enoch. Welcome. Forgive me if I did not greet you warmly. We live with a certain amount of apprehension, knowing that the evil one ever wills our destruction."

"We seek a home here. Would it be possible for us to speak to your husband?" Adriel came directly to the point. *So like him,* Shaina thought, smiling to herself.

"He will be in from the gardens shortly for his noon meal. Please allow your horses to graze, and find a spot in the shade while I bring something to refresh you." The woman hurried inside and returned with a jug of juice, from which she served them. She smiled shyly at Shaina as the dark liquid bubbled into her cup. "Perhaps, when your husband works in the fields, you will bring your grain to grind and will speak of your journey."

Shaina blushed furiously, the rosy color tinging golden skin across high cheekbones. "I am not Adriel's wife, but his niece. He is the youngest brother of my father. We have traveled many miles, and it will be a treat indeed to speak with another woman." She felt her uncle's amused gaze upon her and blushed again.

When Enoch arrived they sat about an outdoor table overlooking the valley, and, while they ate the simple foods set before them, Adriel told the story of Havilah's destruction, his stay with Nathan, and the subsequent journey.

The patriarch's strong, angular face grew troubled at the story, and he spoke sadly at its close. "Sepp and Abigail were among the staunchest of God's people, and Havilah was a stronghold of the Lord. I mourn its passing. You have done well in coming here. So far we have not been molested. Perhaps the evil ones have not discovered us. Or perhaps they simply bide their time. It little matters, I suspect, except each day we're spared allows us time to give the warning to those who will heed it.

"But let us speak now of happier things." Enoch lifted his head and smiled, and the radiance warmed Shaina like the comfort of her mother's arms in childhood. It cut through the grim sorrow she'd lugged across miles and miles of forest, and kindled a flame of hope within her.

"Shaina left her betrothed, her parents, her life of ease and prosperity to become God's child. She has accepted every hardship with patience and courage. I am proud to be her kinsman," Adriel said, turning toward her.

Shaina thought for a moment that she would cry at the kindness in his words, but looking at Enoch, she carefully controlled her emotions. "Thank you for welcoming us into this haven you have prepared. I am a most inexperienced follower of the great God of heaven, but I wish to be faithful and to walk in the footsteps of my grandmother, Abigail."

Enoch sobered and looked at her long and searchingly. "Many have come here with that same desire, child. Only a few remain. It is more difficult for you who have grown up in the world outside. May God help you."

All the warm anticipation drained from her, and a bleakness worse than death flooded her heart. As though he understood, Enoch said kindly, "I will pray for you."

He sat quietly then, thinking, as Rimona cleared away the remains of her meal. Finally, pointing toward an outcropping of rock jutting from the hillside above and beyond them, he turned to Adriel.

"There is a cave above that outcropping that overlooks the valley. Because it faces south, it is warm and sunlit, a pleasant place. Since it was vacated only days ago by a man who chafed at our simple life here, I would suggest it as a comfortable home for Shaina." His gaze shifted to Ira. "I note your tender regard for the young woman. Set up your tent beside her dwelling, and before long you will have built a strong shelter. I trust her to your care. Adriel, son of Sepp, make your dwelling among my sons. I can use a man with the courage to set off into the wilderness with only his God to lead. Perhaps you will travel with me now and again back to the cities to preach."

"I would be honored." Adriel's sad eyes responded to the invitation. "Life means little to me anymore outside of my love for the Promised One. I will never see my dear ones again."

"Oh, my brother, have you borne such a hopeless grief all these miles?" Enoch scanned the man's haggard face in pity. "Let me tell you the good news. The Promised One will come not once, but twice. The first time He will die for us,[1] the second He will return in glory as a mighty Ruler, to raise His dead and take His people home.[2] They sleep, your loved ones, in peace, as shall you and I, if we are faithful, until His blessed voice stirs our graves." [3]

"And how do you know this?" Ira asked quietly. "It is a message new to us."

Humbly, reverently, Enoch explained, his voice strong with the same assurance they'd heard that day at the city well. "He showed me. He showed the great, shining glory of His second appearing.[4] I too was often troubled about the dead, and I pleaded with God for answers.

Early one morning, as I wrestled with these fears, He revealed His solution to sin, and I was satisfied that He is just and loving and wise. We can safely trust in Him. Although He cannot tolerate evil, yet He loves us and will not leave us to the ultimate, inevitable results of human rebellion and sin. He will provide, through the Promised One, an escape for all who desire it. It is hard to believe, but so magnetic is the pull of evil that only a few wish to avail themselves of His rescue,[5] but for those few, the joy is unsurpassed, for what He offers meets the deepest needs of our being in a way that even the pleasures of sin never can. O that I could make that clear to those so intent upon destruction in the cities. It is as though they see only my lips moving but hear nothing. Sometimes, when I am traveling from place to place, I begin to wonder if *I* am mad, for my message falls upon the listeners like so much foolishness. But then, finally, riding home through the deep forests, I feel His presence, and sometimes His messengers travel alongside and encourage and instruct me. Then I know that the words of truth will *always* be foolishness[6] to those cut off from Him. I grieve for my fellow human beings and resolve to go back again and again, searching for those with humble, teachable hearts."

"You are a brave man. Your mission is a dangerous one." Shaina heard the respect in old Ira's voice.

"Not so terribly, my friend. Were I wealthy, they would seize my possessions, but I carry only a message, which they see as neither dangerous nor desirable. At best I glean only an occasional convert who often returns to them at some later date. This valley is yet too far from civilization to tempt them, but the day will come, as mankind multiplies, when we shall *all* fear for our lives."

They separated then, Enoch to return to his crops, the travelers to settle into their new homes. Shaina looked about the cave and thought of her mother's horror could she see her daughter's final destination. Yet the young woman found it a welcome haven—a place to herself after weeks of traveling with inconvenience and lack of privacy. She broke off a long branch of an evergreen and swept away the debris of the former occupant. Rimona gave her armfuls of dried meadow grass to scatter upon the floor. She laid, in one corner, a luxurious fur rug her father had bound upon Hadesh that sad morning of departure. There she would sleep.

The cave angled back into the hillside in such a way that she had total privacy in her sleeping area, and she felt a housewifely satisfaction as she settled her few belongings. On one of the narrow rock shelves that jutted naturally from the cave's interior she placed the blue clay comb with its delicate flowers. Her mother had once promised that she might wear it at her wedding.

Thoughts of Ben flooded her mind, and the cave and its surroundings suddenly seemed as bleak as all the uncharted forests of the earth. She was trapped in this valley and could never find her way back alone. Ben was lost to her forever. A longing to fling herself upon the soft fur of her bed and weep threatened to overwhelm her. Tears streaming down her face, she turned toward an opening in the back of the cave. Following a narrow tunnel that angled sharply at one point, she came out into a sunlit, grassy enclosure surrounded totally by rock walls. Through her tears, Shaina gasped at its possibilities. Instantly she knew why Enoch had given her the cave. Here in this hidden spot she would find the God of Adam and Abigail. This God who had cost her everything. Falling upon her knees, she let the sun soak into her weary, grieving body. Later she would talk to God. Now she would simply be still and heal, letting her posture assure Him that her moment of regret was past, that she was His, no matter the price. But as she knelt a wondrous peace filled her, and she sensed a love beyond that of human lovers. A divine love that left always something more to be explored. A love that demanded, but also fulfilled. A love that nurtured and never destroyed. She sensed that love was present in this valley in a marked way. Instead of being trapped, she had been freed. Love taught her all this in the quiet, sunny nook. Finally she slept, curled on the soft, warm grass, until the sun lowered in the west and left her shivering.

Later she brought Ira to see her discovery, and he said, "It is here that we will plant Adam's daffodils."

"You brought them?" Shaina asked, wide-eyed and unbelieving.

He nodded, pleased at her delight. "Of course, and many other seeds and bulbs. We will make this valley like the garden of the Lord."

In the evening, when Shaina and Ira sat in the front of the cave talking, Adriel scrambled up the hillside to join them.

"Everyone has been warm and welcoming, but when darkness falls, I need my old friends," he stated, seating himself cross-legged beside Ira.

Moonlight glittered on something in his hands, and Shaina teased lightly, "What gift is this you bring us on your first visit?"

"It is only my flute, and I bring you but the humble gift of music."

"Did *everyone* at Havilah play an instrument?" Shaina asked.

"Just about. Father was a real musician, and he insisted that all his sons know the basics. Perhaps Nathan and I enjoyed it more than some of the others. Sepp taught Ben and me to play the flute during our long stints of herding." It was the first time he had spoken of loved ones left behind, and Shaina felt somehow comforted to hear those familiar names once more.

When Adriel lifted the flute to his lips, Shaina was not surprised to hear the plaintive notes of the song of Eve, for it was the song of Havilah, also. Its wistful message drifted over the darkening valley like a lonely cry, and to Shaina it was the distilled sorrow of all mankind awaiting the healing of the Promised One.

* * * * *

During the days ahead the three settled into the routines of the valley. They planted a big garden and tended it meticulously. When they weren't in the garden, they helped with communal grain crops and worked at preparing themselves homes. Adriel built a house of wood, but Ira constructed a shelter of stone that blended so naturally into the hillside it seemed to have grown there. Inside, it contained four rooms, for he knew the cave would be chilly and he wanted room for Shaina to live comfortably with him when the time came. He hollowed out a fire hole in the back wall for warmth, and the other inhabitants of the valley began to climb the hillside to see the remarkable structure. Slowly Shaina came to know them all.

Old Amos, who had played with Seth as a boy; beautiful Mahira and her husband, who had heard Enoch preaching on a city street and left all behind; the sons and daughters of Enoch and Rimona, some, like Methuselah, godly and kind, others resisting and restless. Some married, some lonely and bitter because the valley offered little choice of companions. It wasn't Eden. Sin and sorrow intermingled with true holiness. Only the righteous Enoch held it all together with his pure life and his loving counsel. Often he would leave the encampment for several days at a time, only to return with his face shining and such a sense of peace and joy radiating from him that the others could hardly look at him. They knew he had brushed the very robes of God, and a sacred awe pervaded the valley for days, as though he'd brought them each a gift of holiness. Shaina envied him that divine relationship and sought more and more to approach God herself. In her place of prayer behind the cave, she sought God, and He stooped low to touch the faithful daughter of Nathan and Ona.

When, weeks later, Adriel sat with Ira and Shaina in the bright firelight of Ira's snug stone house, they were totally unprepared for his announcement. "Tomorrow I shall leave with Enoch on a trip to the cities of the plains. He wishes Methuselah to stay here as leader in his place, and thus he has chosen me for his traveling companion. Although I am honored, yet I am a little afraid. I have grown used to the rhythms of this valley, to its solitude and holy peace. Thus I am not sure how well I shall adapt once more to the bombardment of evil in the gathering places of men. It is possible I shall see Nathan, Shaina, and be able to assure him that you are safe and content."

They talked long into the night, she pressing upon him the messages of love she wished conveyed to her parents. Before he left, they knelt on the lip of rock above the moonlit valley and prayed for his and Enoch's safety, and for a purity of soul that would ready them all for the coming of the Promised One.

Next morning, with a sense of unexpected loneliness, she watched the two riders disappear through the slot in the cliff. Enoch was often away, but the valley without Adriel was a new experience, and she turned toward the cave, knowing the weeks ahead would be long ones.

Ira, sensing her mood, called from his doorstep, "Shaina, I have an idea." She walked through the grass, still wet from the morning mist, toward his stone house, wondering what her old friend could have possibly thought up to distract her from Adriel's absence. He held a worn leather pouch, which she recognized as his bulb carrier from her childhood days. "The time has come for us to do some planting. The bulbs must be in the ground through the cold season if they are to bloom in the spring, and there are seeds which should also be planted now for an early start. Our houses are built, our gardens harvested. We must think about beautifying the valley."

"Perhaps life is too serious for us to be concerned about such frivolous things as flowers," she said, still despondent.

"Nonsense. The Lord made Eden splendid, knowing as He did that Adam would soon distrust Him and rebel. Abigail planted an entire hillside to the glory of God, and you yourself have always had a special spot, exquisitely landscaped, in which to worship God, so let me hear no more of this foolishness about frivolity. First, we will plant the daffodils from Eden in your hidden courtyard, then we will walk the length of the valley and begin to formulate a long-range plan. I have been doing some exploring to the north in an area where I suspect no one has ever set foot. There I have seen shrubs and flowers new to both of us. Tomorrow you must join me, and we will begin to bring back a few shrubs at a time, also seeds from those strange new flowers. I am excited already," the old gardener chortled, a gleam in his faded blue eyes.

"And your enthusiasm is contagious, just as you planned it," Shaina laughed. "When Adriel returns, the valley will be awash with color, and my gift to Enoch shall be a bunch of daffodils from Eden valley. He would like that, wouldn't he?"

And so, together, through the cool months, the two explored and dug and planted. They cleaned away brush, mended wooden fences, planted bulbs randomly on sunny hillsides, built stone retaining walls, and at night slept soundly, their bodies pleasantly weary with the day's labor. Slowly the inhabitants of the valley began to take an interest, laying aside their little grievances to help in the undertaking.

Sometimes in the evenings Shaina went to sit with Rimona. She had come to love the gentle woman who moved so quietly about in the home of Enoch, her black hair pulled smoothly back in a knot. Small tendrils escaped and curled about her oval face with its clear ivory skin. Her dark eyes were round and expressive, her body slim and supple. She never seemed hurried, yet her movements were quick and sure.

"You must be very lonely when Enoch goes on these journeys," Shaina sympathized as she shelled nuts before a crackling fire.

"At first, when the children were small, I was not only lonely but afraid. We were alone, here in the valley then, except for Amos, who came soon after we arrived. It was then I really learned to pray. Perhaps, had I not known that fear, I would have ever walked in the shadow of Enoch's experience, but those dark and quiet nights after the children were asleep, I'd kneel here by the fire and talk with God until He became as real to me as my own father had been. Gradually I came to understand that I was totally safe in His keeping.[7] Not that no trouble could ever touch us, but no trouble that had not passed His scrutiny. You do understand the difference?"

"I think so," the younger woman answered, "though I've never thought much about it. You are saying that sometimes we need trouble in order to grow, and so God allows it?"

"It's not a punishment, Shaina. Often people are confused about this. But if we accept trouble with total trust, God can use it to teach us more about Himself.[8] I once thought Enoch's single-minded service to God was a bitter burden, but after I stopped fighting it, I found that the months alone here in the valley were the times I grew closest to Yahweh. Then, instead of driving us apart, his trips knit us together, for he has found in me one who understands his mission and allows him freedom to serve. When he returns, he tells me of the joys and heartaches of his travels, and I speak to him of new depths of holy relationship. Sometimes he takes me by the shoulders and says, "Oh, Mona, what a woman you are! With God for my friend and you for my wife, I am the most blessed of men."

Standing and stretching, Shaina shook the nut shells from her skirt into the fire.

"Are *you* lonely?" the older woman asked, glancing up at the tall girl from the low stool on which she sat.

"Not exactly lonely," she smiled. "It just seems I'm always waiting for something. But I too have learned to find my joy in the Lord and am usually content. I try not to dwell upon my former life. Day by day I've come to understand that Ben could never have brought me happiness."

"We have sons," Rimona hinted, "and they think you are very lovely indeed."

Shaina grinned at her matchmaking. "Dear friend, when God finds a partner for me, He will alert me. This time I shall wait for His signal. Perhaps it is not in His plan. Maybe I shall live out my days here in quietness and whatever service I'm able to render."

They said good night, and Shaina walked briskly in the crisp night air along the valley floor, then sharply upward toward the stone house upon its rocky perch.

*   *   *   *   *

Months later, when the cherry trees were frothy on the hillsides and tulips and jonquils tumbled along stone walls, Enoch, Adriel, and a stranger rode through the slot and down the path into the valley. Shaina, shaking her fur rug high on her rocky perch, was the first to see them. Adriel lifted his hand in greeting, and only then did she acknowledge to herself how bleak the valley had been without his strong, sure presence. By the time she and Ira had clambered down the hillside, all the rest walked beside the horsemen in a babble of welcome. Enoch caught Rimona up before him on the horse, and her face shone with gladness. His grandchildren scampered and shoved alongside, and his sons and daughters formed a half circle protectively about him.

Adriel rode quietly behind, Ira and Shaina on either side. Shaina thought of the time she had so innocently held his hand in grief, but now she felt a shyness that stayed her from reaching out to him in joy. But she read the pleasure in his eyes and knew he was glad to be back.

When the excitement died down a bit, Enoch introduced to them Tobias, his lone convert. The man looked weary and terribly alone. Shaina thought how high the price to be God's man, and determined to invite him soon to a meal with her and Ira.

"Our brother has left behind his companion and his children, his home and his possessions," Enoch announced, and a murmur of sympathy went through the group.

Amos immediately offered the newcomer a room in which to sleep until he could build a dwelling. Tobias smiled at the warmth of their welcome, but it was more like a grimace in the bitter lines of his face.

"We shall all pray that God will lift the sorrow from your heart, friend," Shaina said softly. "We know the pain." The man looked at her gratefully, but said nothing. She turned then to her kinsman. "Come, Adriel, you must eat with us tonight and tell us of the trip."

"Let me first bathe in the stream and put on fresh garments. I have a story to tell you, Shaina. A sober story, but it can wait until we have eaten."

Uneasy, she questioned, "You saw my parents? All is well with them?"

"I shall speak to you of that later," he replied, a firmness in his voice. But all the while she cooked freshly dug parsnips and cut the crusty rye loaves Rimona had taught her to bake, the apprehension grew within her.

While they ate, Adriel admired the baskets of hanging

flowers that swung from the edge of the cave. He marveled at the vistas of color along the hillsides and said it was healing to his eyes, which had seen nothing but the dim forest trail for weeks. It made all the work worthwhile, and Shaina and Ira basked in his praise, but the fear in her grew until she could barely swallow her food.

When they had cleared the food away and sunlight touched only the highest cliffs on the far side of the valley, Adriel leaned back against the side of the cave and began his story. Over his head a hummingbird moved methodically from flower to flower in the hanging baskets.

"Our travels at one point took us within a day's journey of Havilah. I begged Enoch to take the extra time for us to go there. He did not begrudge the delay, but felt it dangerous for me, feeling sure they would recognize me as a Havilah man and lop off my head without a second thought. However, I convinced him that we could swathe our faces in scarves and pass ourselves off as traders from some distant area. We had ample supplies of these monstrous pecans that grow in abundance here, so much against Enoch's better judgment we entered Havilah as peddlers of pecans. You could never believe, Shaina, what has happened in that valley. What was once peaceful farmlands is now a city teeming with evil. Nothing remains the same, except Mother's hillside gardens, which they have retained as a sort of showpiece. In fact, that flowering hillside was the center of attention when we arrived. It seemed half the city had gathered there, a raucous mob milling about at the foot of the great idol they have erected among the flowers."

Why must he ramble on and on about Havilah. Shaina thought impatiently. *Doesn't he know my heart thirsts for news of my parents?* But she held her peace. She could see Ira was lost in his story.

"No one paid the slightest heed to us," Adriel contin

ued, "so intent were they upon two men being held at spearpoint near the idol. Something about the two, even though their backs were toward us, seemed familiar, and I realized with a sickening feeling that they were Nathan and Ben. Had not Enoch held my arm with an iron grip, I should have leaped toward them, though there was nothing I could have done in that sea of spears. 'They are my kinsmen,' I whispered frantically to Enoch. 'We must do something.'

" 'There is nothing we can do,' he replied calmly, 'except pray that they will meet death as befits men of God.'

"I knew he was right, but I almost hated him momentarily for his detachment. Some city leader, wearing a headpiece of gold, spoke to Nathan and Ben, telling them they were recognized as men of Havilah, and as such were subject to death unless they were willing to prove their disregard for the God of its former inhabitants by kneeling and worshiping the image there before them. A great sadness came over me, for I knew those two sons of Sepp would betray all who had already died by bending the knee before that glittering idol. Ben knelt quickly, his head bowed in an attitude of reverence. Wondering what thoughts were in the mind of this nephew of mine, I wept for his weakness."

Adriel turned, then, to look full at Shaina, whose face was as white as the doves who pecked for crumbs along the cave's overhang. He reached out and took her hand as he went on.

"Nathan just stood there, hesitating, until a spear proded his shoulder, staining his robe with blood. I saw Enoch's lips moving in prayer, and I too pleaded with God for Nathan's victory. Finally your father turned, his face as pale as yours is now, Shaina; but he said in clear, strong tones, 'I cannot kneel before this useless thing here in my mother's gardens dedicated to the Creator of all mankind. I have not served Him faithfully or well, to

SOE-4

my sorrow, but I declare Him today, before this gathering, to be the only true and living God.'

"The words hardly escaped his lips before the mob attacked him with rocks and their fists. No spear had even to be lifted. In moments the crowd began to drift away, their thoughts already upon other matters. Behind them, your father lay still, blending into the very soil with his brown potter's robe and sandy hair. Enoch and I dared not speak or show interest in the event, but as our eyes met we knew a fierce rejoicing even in our sadness."

Shaina wept quietly, cradled protectively against Ira's shoulder. "Oh, Adriel," she said, somehow smiling through her tears. "It is a glorious story. My heart is shattered, but it is yet a glorious story. Oh, that I could have heard him speak those words. Thank you—thank you for telling me."

The three of them wept together then, for father, brother, and loved master. Finally Shaina asked, "What of my mother, Adriel? What will she do without Father? Did you see her?"

"We didn't travel in the direction of your home this journey, Shaina, so we didn't see Ona. But as Ben left the scene of Nathan's death we followed him at some distance until we were well away from the crowds. He and Nathan and the servants had made camp on higher ground above the city. They had come to bargain for clay. As Ben ascended the hillside, we caught up with him and spread our sacks of nuts before him as though in trade. Then I slipped the scarf from my face, and he gasped in disbelief. We dared talk only a few moments, but Ben promised us he would take your mother into his care. He is fond of Ona, and I believe will be a son to her, so you need not fear for her welfare. We gave him all your messages of love for her, and they will comfort her, surely."

"I wish I could go to her," Shaina sighed. "She will be

devastated, partly at his death, and partly because, in the end, he chose his God above her after all."

Adriel picked up his flute, and as he played softly, sadly, Shaina felt the music in new and deeper ways.

[1] "For God so loved the world that he gave his one and only Son, that whoever believes in him shall not perish but have eternal life" (John 3:16).

[2] "Do not let your hearts be troubled. Trust in God; trust also in me. In my Father's house are many rooms; if it were not so, I would have told you. I am going there to prepare a place for you. And if I go and prepare a place for you, I will come back and take you to be with me that you also may be where I am" (John 14:1-3).

"At that time they will see the Son of Man coming in a cloud with power and great glory" (Luke 21:27).

"They were looking intently up into the sky as he was going, when suddenly two men dressed in white stood beside them. 'Men of Galilee,' they said, 'why do you stand here looking into the sky? This same Jesus, who has been taken from you into heaven, will come back in the same way you have seen him go into heaven' " (Acts 1:10, 11).

"Christ was sacrificed once to take away the sins of many people; and he will appear a second time, not to bear sin, but to bring salvation to those who are waiting for him" (Hebrews 9:28).

[3] "Brothers, we do not want you to be ignorant about those who fall asleep, or to grieve like the rest of men, who have no hope" (1 Thessalonians 4:13).

"And if Christ has not been raised, your faith is futile; you are still in your sins. Then those also who have fallen asleep in Christ are lost. If only for this life we have hope in Christ, we are to be pitied more than all men. But Christ has indeed been raised from the dead, the firstfruits of those who have fallen asleep" (1 Corinthians 15:17-20).

"At that time Michael, the great prince who protects your people, will arise. There will be a time of distress such as has not happened from the beginning of nations until then. But at that time your people—everyone whose name is found written in the book—will be delivered. Multitudes who sleep in the dust of the earth will awake: some to everlasting life, others to shame and everlasting contempt" (Daniel 12:1, 2).

"All go to the same place; all come from dust, and to dust all return" (Ecclesiastes 3:20).

"Whatever your hand finds to do, do it with all your might, for in the grave, where you are going, there is neither working nor planning nor knowledge nor wisdom" (Ecclesiastes 9:10).

"For the living know that they will die, but the dead know nothing; they have no further reward, and even the memory of them is forgotten. Their love, their hate and their jealousy have long since vanished; never again will they have a part in anything that happens under the sun" (Ecclesiastes 9:5, 6).

"No one remembers you when he is dead. Who praises you from the grave?" (Psalm 6:5).

"It is not the dead who praise the Lord, those who go down to silence;" (Psalm 115:17).

"For the Lord himself will come down from heaven, with a loud command, with the voice of the archangel and with the trumpet call of God, and the dead in Christ will rise first" (1 Thessalonians 4:16).

"Do not be amazed at this, for a time is coming when all who are in their graves will hear his voice and come out— those who have done good will rise to live, and those who have done evil will rise to be condemned" (John 5:28, 29).

"I have the same hope in God as these men, that there will be a resurrection of both the righteous and the wicked" (Acts 24:15).

"Listen, I tell you a mystery: We will not all sleep, but we will all be changed—in a flash, in the twinkling of an eye, at the last trumpet. For the trumpet will sound, the dead will be raised imperishable, and we will be changed" (1 Corinthians 15:51, 52).

[4] "Enoch, the seventh from Adam, prophesied about these men: 'See, the Lord is coming with thousands of his holy ones to judge everyone, and to convict all the ungodly of all the ungodly acts they have done in the ungodly way, and of all the harsh words ungodly sinners have spoken against him' " (Jude 14, 15).

[5] "Enter through the narrow gate. For wide is the gate and broad is the road that leads to destruction, and many enter through it. But small is the gate and narrow the road that leads

to life, and only a few find it" (Matthew 7:13, 14).

6 "The man without the Spirit does not accept the things that come from the Spirit of God, for they are foolishness to him, and he cannot understand them, because they are spiritually discerned" (1 Corinthians 2:14).

"For the message of the cross is foolishness to those who are perishing, but to us who are being saved it is the power of God" (1 Corinthians 1:18).

7 "A righteous man may have many troubles, but the LORD delivers him from them all" (Psalm 34:19).

"God is our refuge and strength, an ever-present help in trouble" (Psalm 46:1).

"The LORD is a refuge for the oppressed, a stronghold in times of trouble" (Psalm 9:9).

"When you pass through the waters, I will be with you; and when you pass through the rivers, they will not sweep over you. When you walk through the fire, you will not be burned; the flames will not set you ablaze" (Isaiah 43:2).

"The LORD is my shepherd, I shall not be in want. He makes me lie down in green pastures, he leads me beside quiet waters, he restores my soul. He guides me in paths of righteousness for his name's sake. Even though I walk through the valley of the shadow of death, I will fear no evil, for you are with me; your rod and your staff, they comfort me" (Psalm 23:1-4).

8 "Not only so, but we also rejoice in our sufferings, because we know that suffering produces perseverance; perseverance, character; and character, hope. And hope does not disappoint us, because God has poured out his love into our hearts by the Holy Spirit, whom he has given us" (Romans 5:3-5).

"Our fathers disciplined us for a little while as they thought best; but God disciplines us for our good, that we may share in his holiness" (Hebrews 12:10).

"Blessed is the man who perseveres under trial, because when he has stood the test, he will receive the crown of life that God has promised to those who love him" (James 1:12).

THE DEPARTURE

Rimona made life possible in the remote valley. She knew everything that grew in it and for miles around, knew what roots and wild plants would cure their rare illnesses. From the silky hair of the goat as well as the fleece of the sheep she could weave fine clothing and could shape a strong and lasting clay pot. As the years passed, Shaina proved an eager pupil, but in nothing so much as in the working of clay. From childhood, Shaina had played with it upon the floor of her father's shop, but she had never worked with it seriously. Now as she learned the techniques, often turning the wheel upon which Rimona formed her creations, she became fascinated and soon had Ira turning one for her as she shaped the wet clay into useful forms. But she could not stop with plain utensils. Her clever fingers soon fashioned flowers and vines to decorate the practical pieces, and then, later, came the shapes of birds and deer and even the likenesses of men and women. With her flowers and her clay she brought a sense of the beautiful into their Spartan lives once more, and the valley was better for her presence.

Often at sundown at the beginning of the Sabbath day, Shaina invited all the inhabitants of the valley up to the great lip of rock on which the cave rested, for the sunset was spectacular from there. Ira built a handsome altar to one side of the cave's mouth on which Enoch might make sacrifice for all the people week by week. They formed the habit of confessing any wrongs they'd done one another and of settling their private sins in a session of sober, silent prayer before the sacred rite.[1] Only then did Enoch slay the lamb. Because it was a small place, they recognized and loved individually even the animals. Thus, when a sheep waited innocently beside the altar, often a lamb one had held and petted during the week, it was a moment of poignant sadness when Enoch raised the knife. Afterward, sometimes, Adriel played his flute and they sang together, but often so intense was the feeling of sacredness there that they just left quietly, loath to break the silence.

Then, on seventh day, the Sabbath, they gathered by the clear pool at the foot of the mountain stream to sing and pray together before Enoch spoke to them. Shaina loved to watch his face. Sometimes he told the stories that Adam had shared with him of Creation and those first fair days in Eden. He recounted their joy as they explored every wonder fresh from the Creator's hand, and the fear and sorrow Adam felt as he saw Eve approaching with the forbidden fruit in her hands and all the eager rationalizations upon her lips.[2]

As he talked, Shaina visualized Eden valley, and saw the sad, beautiful face of Eve as she sang, with Nathan's harp, the story of her loss and pain.[3]

At other times Enoch shared the revelation God had given him of a great calamity to afflict the earth, then later of the coming of the Promised One to die. And the story they loved best of all, the great, glorious second coming of God's Promised One.[4] No matter how many times he told them his revelations, they never tired of them, for each week he knit the immeasurable love of God so tenderly, so uniquely, into it that they longed to know more of that wise and wonderful God who cared for them.

It seemed each week that Enoch's relationship intensified until, as he walked among them, the very presence of God was in their midst. They wished that he would not go on his short journeys alone into the wilderness to pray, and certainly not on those long, dangerous travels among the descendants of Cain. But they knew he must, that he was God's man, and that they were blessed to be sheep of his flock.

Shaina noted often that Tobias never smiled, and no matter how warmly the others drew him into their fellowship, he never seemed a part of them. One seventh day, as she climbed high among the cliffs, she came upon him huddled in a crevice, weeping. Startled, she hardly knew whether to pretend she had not seen him or to speak, but chose the latter alternative as the totally honest one.

"Tobias, I have noticed your sadness. What can we do to help you?"

He laughed bitterly. "Get me out of this place. Take me back to civilization."

"Do you fear that your wife and children are in need?"

"My wife was about to leave me anyhow. She was the child of wealth and hated my worship of God, though it didn't seem to bother her when we fell in love. She was packing to go back to her home when Enoch came along preaching his message of doom. It seemed nothing mattered. Since I was losing everything anyhow, I figured I might as well join him. By the time I'd traveled a few weeks through that endless forest, I knew I'd made a terrible mistake. I hate it here. And I don't intend to live out my life without a woman, either."

"I understand your feelings." Shaina thought uneasily of the distance between herself and the camp and determined not to get herself into such a situation again. "Sometimes I too am lonely, but I try to fill my time with useful activities, to remember that this life is not important. There will be a life with God later on that will meet all our needs.[5] But even here and now, Tobias, if you open your heart to God, He will so fill you with His presence that you will have joy even in this remote place." [6]

The dark, brooding man made no reply, seeming to withdraw even deeper into the crevice. Shaina, unable to think of anything else to say, began her slow, careful descent of the mountainside, ever aware of his eyes upon her. She felt soiled somehow, and wished she had not encountered him.

That night, when she saw Adriel climbing upward toward her cave, she was pleased, for she had a surprise for him. After they chatted a bit, she went inside the cave and returned with her hands behind her back.

"Shut your eyes, Adriel. All winter I have been making a gift for you. It is finally complete, and I can hardly wait to show it to you."

Adriel, seated on a bench at the cave's entrance, leaned back against the rocky wall and held out his hands. Shaina noted as his head rested, relaxed, against the gray stone, eyes closed, that the lines of suffering and sorrow that had so long etched his face had begun to soften. He looked, there in the soft twilight, surprisingly young and vulnerable. She felt a wave of tenderness wash over her, but she brushed it aside hastily, placing in his hands a long object in a soft deerskin bag.

Adriel pulled at the lacing, smiling, gently amused and more touched than he cared to admit. What he drew from the bag caused him to gasp in wonder. Shaina, using many varied hues of clay, had fashioned a miniature Havilah. The tents of Sepp and Abigail sprawled in their proper spot, tiny sheep dotted hillside meadows, and the river wound in and out among the fields and trees. Abigail bent industriously in her vegetable gardens behind the cooking tent, and Shaina had formed the figure of Sepp so perfectly, standing, lamb in hand, by his altar, his long, thick hair lifted slightly by the wind, that Adriel caressed it lovingly with a pensive forefinger.

When he looked up at last, his eyes were full of tears. Had he not spoken at all, Shaina would have been amply repaid for her painstaking work, but, brokenly his words reached out to her.

"Oh, Shaina, what a beautiful thing you have done. When our memories grow old and dim, this work of your hands will remind us still of our heritage. Havilah, as it was, will never die." He patted the bench beside him, inviting her to sit down. Gently he took her hand, and they sat together in the dusk, not speaking, but feeling something natural and good, something strong and everlasting, moving between them. Finally, in his simple, unadorned way, he told her, "Shaina, I have grown to love you so very much, but I have been afraid to speak."

"What did you fear?" the young woman asked, too shy now to look into his face.

"That I am older than you, that you could think of me only as a kinsman and not a lover. And most of all, perhaps, that your heart still belonged to Ben."

"I feel more for you now, in this moment," she said softly, raising her eyes timidly to his face, "than I felt for Ben ever. I know now that my love for him was shallow and untried. You and I, Adriel, have walked together in sorrow, faced together a new life, and waited patiently for our love to ripen."

"Not so patiently as you might think," he confessed, grinning. "A thousand times I've longed to take you in my arms, to be warmed and comforted by your love."

"I too have felt that same need," she admitted. "And it is not necessary to deny it longer." She opened her arms, and he turned into them. As she held him, their tears mingled and their terrible loneliness fell away like an outgrown garment.

* * * * *

Rimona and Shaina planned such a celebration as the valley had never seen. Shaina wanted her wedding to be a time of rejoicing, yet a sacred, holy experience as well.

She wished each of the couples in the valley to be reminded of their own vows of faithfulness, for their love to be renewed.

For days the women cooked, preparing fruit breads and other delicacies from the abundance growing about them. Rimona took her softest cloth, made from the fine combed hair of goats, and dipped it in onionskin dyes. The resulting fabric was a warm gold, only a shade lighter than Shaina's bronzed skin. When she slipped into it on her wedding day, her mother's blue comb tucked into her coppery hair, Rimona let out a long sigh of satisfaction. The children wove chains of tiny blue flowers for her neck, and the bridal procession set off down the valley. Shaina had made Adriel go far down the long path to a desolate area of steep rocks.

"Only when you hear the sound of our singing may you come to meet us," she had warned, teasing, her green eyes dancing.

Through the early morning they came, sunlight dappling the well-trodden path beneath great trees. Shaina walked slowly, proudly, like a queen in her happiness, between Enoch and Rimona, their spiritual child. About them the children danced and tossed flowers. Behind followed the rest, and their songs of praise and gratitude to God rose triumphant in the hidden valley so far removed from the dwellings of humanity.

They rounded a bend, and Adriel walked to meet them, playing his flute. The group halted and became silent, letting the joyful notes of his song of love fall clear and sweet on the morning air. Shaina saw in his eyes his loyalty, his love, and his appreciation of her beauty as he stood before her, fingering his flute with consummate skill. He turned then and led them down a side path to the little clearing that they had chosen in which to pledge themselves to one another.

She would always remember this moment, she thought. The mighty strength of Adriel going before them, the music of his ecstasy dancing behind him along the woodland path and over the heads of God's faithful children. She wondered what sorrows awaited them all, what dangers hovered about his head as he traveled often with Enoch over the earth in search of others. Would she lose him someday, this steady, true man of Havilah? She pushed her forebodings aside and made herself absorb all the happiness of the hour.

They took their place beneath a wisteria tree, hanging thick with its purple bloom. There, with bees buzzing above their heads, Enoch spoke to them soberly of the sacredness of marriage and of that first union in Eden.[7] Then they all knelt in the soft grass where deep-blue flax, which Shaina and Ira had planted years before, crowded in upon them, and Shaina's golden dress glowed like a live flame in the midst of it. Enoch placed a hand upon each of their heads and solemnly beseeched God to bind their lives together for all time. Many prayers then followed, unhurried and sincere, each seeking blessings upon the two. Little children lisped their petitions, their friendship with God as natural as their breathing.

Lastly Adriel prayed, a pledge of enduring love for his bride before the Creator of the world, and lifting her up, he carried her homeward along the path, her arms about his neck, her slight body light as thistledown in his strong arms, the golden dress fluttering brightly in the morning breeze.

They feasted and laughed and sang. Shaina noted Enoch pausing often to draw Rimona to him, kissing her playfully before the guests, making her blush with pleasure. *What a complex man he is,* she thought to herself. Stern prophet warning fearlessly the sons of Cain, radiant friend of God, tender, attentive mate and father. She hoped God was like Enoch. It would make Him so easy to love. *No,* she told herself, *God is even more than Enoch.*

When the sun had at last vanished behind the hills and not even the highest cliffs reflected its warmth, Shaina and Adriel climbed hand in hand toward the cave. Behind them friends sang a song of love as old as Eden:

> Lift up my beloved
> and carry her gently
> to the place of my resting.
> She is wondrously fair,
> my beloved.
> My heart leaps
> at her touch,
> And darkness covers us.

* * * * *

A few months later, as the Sabbath day service ended, Enoch invited Shaina and Adriel to join him as he journeyed north of the valley for a time of solitary prayer and meditation. Since the patriarch seldom took anyone except Rimona or Methuselah, and them only on rare occasions, the couple felt deeply honored. They hurried home to gather up a few necessities for the journey, and set out on foot through the wild terrain that Ira and Shaina often traversed searching for new plants.

Enoch spoke to them of things to come more intensely than ever before. "Adriel," he cautioned, "God's men grow few upon the earth, though He does have some scattered here and there.[8] When I am gone, you and Methuselah and those of my sons who remain faithful to God must continue to warn men of the annihilation to come.[9] Beg them to forsake evil and return to God. Promise me, Adriel."

Shaina's husband looked at his friend curiously. "You are a young man, not yet 400, Enoch.[10] The destruction may well come long before you sleep in the earth. I doubt that Methuselah or I will ever have to take over your work, though you know we will travel beside you whatever the risk."

"But you will promise? Methuselah has already solemnly sworn to carry on."

"I promise," Adriel vowed soberly, aware that it was, for some reason, extremely important to Enoch. Shaina, walking behind them along the rocky path, wondered at the conversation. Enoch strode before them in the full strength of his manhood, magnetic and powerful.

He led them, after a day's journey, into a small desolate clearing among great rocks. From it one could gaze out across mountains and valleys into lands not yet inhabited.

"Why do you come to such a forsaken spot to pray?" Shaina asked, feeling the awesome loneliness of the place.

"Because here I sense my insignificance. In the city, or even in our valley, anywhere people congregate, we get to thinking we are vital to the scheme of things, but here, alone, I am ever aware that God could eliminate me, or all of us, with but a single thought. And I am overwhelmed with His divine tolerance toward a rebellious people. I am aware of my own unworthiness and His compassionate love for me. I think of my strong parental devotion toward my sons and daughters and what it would cost me to send one of them on such a mission as God will assign the Promised One on this earth.[11] Only here, alone upon my knees, do I begin to glimpse the incomprehensible depth of His love. Now, let us speak no more and seek His presence."

They separated, each finding his private nook. Shaina felt overwhelmed. What did she know of seeking God alongside such a holy man, or even her own husband, for that matter? Many a night after Adriel thought her asleep, she'd heard him slip from their bed and go through the tunnel to their place of prayer. But she knelt and waited quietly. Perhaps the Lord would speak to her, as He had sent His peace that first day in the valley. The vast quietness settled upon her, and she tried to imagine what it would be like to be here alone as Enoch was so often. She strove to empty her mind of thought, until at last she lost all sense of her surroundings, the pain in her knees upon hard rock, the awareness of her fellow worshipers. Although she heard no divine voice, saw no glory, a healing warmth flowed into her, which she recognized as acceptance, God's acceptance of her offering of self. It was as real as the stone upon which she knelt, and she wept with gratitude that God would meet her in this place and communicate with her. A great longing to offer Him something better surged within her.

When darkness fell, Adriel came and lifted her up and held her close within the folds of their woolen blanket, but they did not speak, so strong was the power of God upon them.

* * * * *

As dawn sent its warming rays over the sleeping couple, the hunched, damp form of Enoch rose from a kneeling position beside a gray boulder. Waking, Shaina realized he must have been there all night, and she arose quickly to prepare hot food for him, but there was something strange about the man, a glow surrounding him not unlike the flaming glory of Eden. Shaina covered her face with her arm and awakened her husband, who sat up in wonder at the sight. As the light grew brighter, the form of Enoch began to recede. He smiled at them, the same old kindly, radiant smile, and he spoke, looking fiercely at Adriel.

"The promise, Adriel. Remember the promise."

The younger man reached out as though to detain him, but the light flashed and blazed, and then all was as before, except that Enoch was gone.[12]

Adriel and Shaina stared at each other in utter astonishment. "He will return," Shaina assured her husband. "I must prepare food for him. He was all night in prayer."

Her husband pulled her back down beside him. "No, my love, he will not return. God has taken him from us. The world is a dark place, indeed, without his presence, but we must take up his work as best we can."

She looked at the dry area of rock where the mist had fallen all about Enoch and tried to realize that her flesh-and-blood friend had entered the very presence of God.

"This is holy ground, Adriel, and we have seen a sacred thing this day. Enoch knew when he brought us, didn't he? We are so close to heaven that it frightens me. We think we are so far from God that we can live our own lives and think our own thoughts, but He's so close He can just reach out and take Enoch from our world into His."

"There's nothing to fear, precious one." He put his arms about her protectively. "The arms of God are safer than mine. I think God just wanted us to know how close He really is, and He also wanted us to see, through Enoch's experience, that someday, when the Promised One has paid the terrible price, He will return and take those who love Him home with Him, just as He did our friend. He wants us to know this bleak existence isn't forever, and that beyond lies the glorious life of Eden once more."

They clung together, awed and silent by what they had just experienced. When Adriel spoke again, his voice was more sober than Shaina had ever heard it. "We must go home now, Shaina, and I will talk with Methuselah about our assignment. You and I shall be apart much more, dear one, than before, and the dangers of our lives will increase. Once the descendants of Cain hear that Enoch is gone, they will become more bold. His godliness placed a restraint upon them."

As they walked hand in hand back through the wild places, they did not talk much, but each knew the other's thoughts. The sadness of separation rested heavily upon them, the miraculous event astonished them, and they wondered how to tell Rimona.

"She loved him so much," Shaina sighed. "Will she ever believe our story?"

But when they came down the trail into the valley, Rimona, with her children, walked to meet them and, holding out her hands, she said, "I know. I know." Enoch had told his family, and said his farewells before he left. Sorrow walked among them, but Rimona held her head high. "It isn't every woman whose husband dwells with God," she smiled, and Shaina thought that Deity must surely treasure such a one as this.

That evening, as Methuselah led out in worship, he asked Adriel to tell the story of Enoch's leave-taking from the world. Some murmured their disbelief, some hinted of foul play, but Rimona stood beside Adriel and confirmed his story. In the end, all knelt with a deep sense of need, to ask God's continued leadership among them. And they all knew nothing would ever be quite the same again.

[1] "Therefore confess your sins to each other and pray for each other so that you may be healed. The prayer of a righteous man is powerful and effective" (James 5:16).

[2] "Now the serpent was more crafty than any of the wild animals the LORD God had made. He said to the woman, 'Did God really say, "You must not eat from any tree in the garden"?' The woman said to the serpent, 'We may eat fruit from the trees in the garden, but God did say, "You must not eat fruit from the tree that is in the middle of the garden, and you must not touch it, or you will die." ' 'You will not surely die,' the serpent said to the woman. 'For God knows that when you eat of it your eyes will be opened, and you will be like God, knowing good and evil.' When the woman saw that the fruit of the tree was good for food and pleasing to the eye, and also

desirable for gaining wisdom, she took some and ate it. She also gave some to her husband, who was with her, and he ate it. Then the eyes of both of them were opened, and they realized they were naked; so they sewed fig leaves together and made coverings for themselves. Then the man and his wife heard the sound of the LORD God as he was walking in the garden in the cool of the day, and they hid from the LORD God among the trees of the garden. But the LORD God called to the man, 'Where are you?' He answered, 'I heard you in the garden, and I was afraid because I was naked; so I hid,' And he said, 'Who told you that you were naked? Have you eaten from the tree that I commanded you not to eat from?' The man said, 'The woman you put here with me—she gave me some fruit from the tree, and I ate it.' Then the LORD God said to the woman, 'What is this you have done?' The woman said, 'The serpent deceived me, and I ate' " (Genesis 3:1-13).

[3] "So the LORD God said to the serpent, 'Because you have done this, cursed are you above all the livestock and all the wild animals! You will crawl on your belly and you will eat dust all the days of your life. And I will put enmity between you and the woman, and between your offspring and hers; he will crush your head, and you will strike his heel.' To the woman he said, 'I will greatly increase your pains in childbearing; with pain you will give birth to children. Your desire will be for your husband, and he will rule over you.' To Adam he said, 'Because you listened to your wife and ate from the tree about which I commanded you, "You must not eat of it," Cursed is the ground because of you; through painful toil you will eat of it all the days of your life. It will produce thorns and thistles for you, and you will eat the plants of the field. By the sweat of your brow you will eat your food until you return to the ground, since from it you were taken; for dust you are and to dust you will return.' Adam named his wife Eve, because she would become the mother of all the living. The LORD God made garments of skin for Adam and his wife and clothed them. And the LORD God said, 'The man has now become like one of us, knowing good and evil. He must not be allowed to reach out his hand and take also from the tree of life and eat, and live forever.' So the LORD God banished him from the Garden of Eden to work the ground from which he had been taken. After he drove the man out, he placed on the east side of the Garden

of Eden cherubim and a flaming sword flashing back and forth to guard the way to the tree of life" (Genesis 3:14-24).

⁴ "Enoch, the seventh from Adam, prophesied about these men: 'See, the Lord is coming with thousands upon thousands of his holy ones to judge everyone, and to convict all the ungodly of all the ungodly acts they have done in the ungodly way, and of all the harsh words ungodly sinners have spoken against him' " (Jude 14, 15).

⁵ "Behold, I will create new heavens and a new earth. The former things will not be remembered, nor will they come to mind" (Isaiah 65:17).

"But in keeping with his promise we are looking forward to a new heaven and a new earth, the home of righteousness" (2 Peter 3:13).

"Then I saw a new heaven and a new earth, for the first heaven and the first earth had passed away, and there was no longer any sea. I saw the Holy City, the new Jerusalem, coming down out of heaven from God, prepared as a bride beautifully dressed for her husband. And I heard a loud voice from the throne saying, 'Now the dwelling of God is with men, and he will live with them. They will be his people, and God himself will be with them and be their God. He will wipe every tear from their eyes. There will be no more death or mourning or crying or pain, for the old order of things has passed away.' He who was seated on the throne said, 'I am making everything new!' Then he said, 'Write this down, for these words are trustworthy and true' " (Revelation 21:1-5).

⁶ "You have made known to me the path of life; you will fill me with joy in your presence, with eternal pleasures at your right hand" (Psalm 16:11)

"Then will I go to the altar of God, to God, my joy and my delight. I will praise you with the harp, O God, my God" (Psalm 43:4).

"Nehemiah said, 'Go and enjoy choice food and sweet drinks, and send some to those who have nothing prepared. This day is sacred to our Lord. Do not grieve, for the joy of the LORD is your strength' " (Nehemiah 8:10).

"May the God of hope fill you with all joy and peace as you trust in him, so that you may overflow with hope by the power of the Holy Spirit" (Romans 15:13).

"And there rejoice before the LORD your God, you, your sons

and daughters, your menservants and maidservants, and the Levites from your towns, who have no allotment or inheritance of their own" (Deuteronomy 12:12).

"Rejoice in the LORD and be glad, you righteous; sing, all you who are upright in heart!" (Psalm 32:11).

"Then my soul will rejoice in the LORD and delight in his salvation" (Psalm 35:9).

"But may all who seek you rejoice and be glad in you; may those who love your salvation always say, 'Let God be exalted!' " (Psalm 70:4).

"My spirit rejoices in God my Savior" (Luke 1:47).

[7] "Then God said, 'Let us make man in our image, in our likeness, and let them rule over the fish of the sea and the birds of the air, over the livestock, over all the earth, and over all the creatures that move along the ground.'

"So God created man in his own image, in the image of God he created him; male and female he created them.

"God blessed them and said to them, 'Be fruitful and increase in number; fill the earth and subdue it. Rule over the fish of the sea and the birds of the air and over every living creature that moves on the ground' " (Genesis 1:26-28).

"So the man gave names to all the livestock, the birds of the air and all the beasts of the field. But for Adam no suitable helper was found. So the LORD God caused the man to fall into a deep sleep; and while he was sleeping, he took one of the man's ribs and closed up the place with flesh. Then the LORD God made a woman from the rib he had taken out of the man, and he brought her to the man. The man said, 'This is now bone of my bones and flesh of my flesh; she shall be called "woman," for she was taken out of man.' For this reason a man will leave his father and mother and be united to his wife, and they will become one flesh. The man and his wife were both naked, and they felt no shame" (Genesis 2:20-25).

[8] "The LORD saw how great man's wickedness on the earth had become, and that every inclination of the thoughts of his heart was only evil all the time" (Genesis 6:5).

[9] "The LORD was grieved that he had made man on the earth, and his heart was filled with pain. So the LORD said, 'I will wipe mankind, whom I have created, from the face of the earth — men and animals, and creatures that move along the ground,

and birds of the air—for I am grieved that I have made them' " (Genesis 6:6, 7).

[10] "When Enoch had lived 65 years, he became the father of Methuselah. And after he became the father of Methuselah, Enoch walked with God 300 years and had other sons and daughters. Altogether, Enoch lived 365 years" (Genesis 5:21-23).

[11] "In the beginning was the Word, and the Word was with God, and the Word was God. He was with God in the beginning.

"Through him all things were made; without him nothing was made that has been made. In him was life, and that life was the light of men. The light shines in the darkness, but the darkness has not understood it. . . . He was in the world, and though the world was made through him, the world did not recognize him. He came to that which was his own, but his own did not receive him. Yet to all who received him, to those who believed in his name, he gave the right to become children of God—children born not of natural descent, nor of human decision or a husband's will, but born of God. The Word became flesh and made his dwelling among us. We have seen his glory, the glory of the One and Only, who came from the Father, full of grace and truth" (John 1:1-14).

"For God so loved the world that he gave his one and only Son, that whoever believes in him shall not perish but have eternal life" (John 3:16).

"For I have come down from heaven not to do my will but to do the will of him who sent me" (John 6:38).

"For the Son of Man came to seek and to save what was lost" (Luke 19:10).

"You see, at just the right time, when we were still power-less, Christ died for the ungodly. Very rarely will anyone die for a righteous man, though for a good man someone might possibly dare to die. But God demonstrates his own love for us in this: While we were still sinners, Christ died for us" (Romans 5:6-8).

"He who did not spare his own Son, but gave him up for us all—how will he not also, along with him, graciously give us all things?" (Romans 8:32).

[12] "And after he became the father of Methuselah, Enoch walked with God 300 years and had other sons and daughters.

Altogether, Enoch lived 365 years. Enoch walked with God; then he was no more, because God took him away" (Genesis 5:22-24).

"By faith Enoch was taken from this life, so that he did not experience death; he could not be found, because God had taken him away. For before he was taken, he was commended as one who pleased God" (Hebrews 11:5).

THE GIRL

Rimona poured grain into the hollow stone as Shaina, with a graceful swaying motion, pounded a worn pestle within a cloud of rising dust. They worked together as one, and only when the younger woman stepped back and pushed her burnished hair from her perspiring face did they move into the shade for a brief rest.

"If Adriel could see you now!" Rimona chuckled, gazing upon Shaina's dusty face, mottled with little rivulets of perspiration.

"He'd love me anyhow," Shaina replied, her heart suddenly filled with longing.

Methuselah and Shaina's husband had set out months before to do Enoch's work, and Shaina, now long used to the journeys, waited in hope, always knowing that one trip or another would be their last. From Rimona she drew strength, and from her she learned to place the worry in God's hands. But she never stopped missing Adriel.

The valley had changed over the 300 years since Enoch's departure. It seemed to Shaina that the righteous had grown more so and the restless more defiant, as though both good and evil had distilled. Tobias had long since ridden away with Methuselah and Adriel, leaving Enoch's refuge with obvious relief. And he was not the only one. Many of Enoch's sons and grandsons ventured into the world beyond the valley, some to nurture faith in their father's God, some to sample rebellion. Lamech, inheritor of the spiritual legacy, did not come and go as did his father and Adriel, but traveled far afield, speaking boldly for God and finally settling on the very fringes of the land of Nod.

Adriel and Shaina, handsome and vigorous in the prime of their lives, knew but one purpose, to further the worship and love of God on earth. And they shared a great joy. After years of barrenness, Shaina had borne a girl child with green eyes and the dark, smoldering beauty of her grandmother Ona. But she had nothing of Ona's capricious nature—only a steady cheerfulness that was ever a wonder to her parents.

"She has my mother's face and Abigail's soul," Shaina often said to Adriel. "Could a child be more blessed?" They named her Navit (Nuh-veet), "the pleasant one," and she was a child of the earth and of the God of Creation.

This day she had gone to sit with an old woman at the far end of the valley who was dying, slipping naturally and peacefully into that last rest to await the call of the Promised One.[1] Navit knew death and birth well, having trotted all of her childhood behind Shaina and Rimona as they rendered their services in such events. Now, at 22, she often attended to the needs of others in every circumstance, and when the elderly ached or could no longer see, it was for Navit they called, to help them while away the long hours with her soothing touch, her ready laughter, and most of all her singing. The music of Havilah was in her, enabling her to play the instruments Adriel brought back to her from the cities and to sing with a voice that moved her listeners to tears. Amos taught her the old, first songs, sung at the gates of Eden, passed down from generation to generation, and Adriel himself taught her the song of Eve with all its pain and pathos.

When Methuselah and Adriel rode at long last, single file, into the valley, a third person accompanied them.

Shaina and Navit, bounding down the hillside, hardly glanced at the shrouded stranger, so great was their joy in greeting the one they loved and had so long awaited. Finally Shaina turned toward the dusty traveler. Adriel watched, a smile upon his tired face, a hint of amusement in his eye.

As Shaina lifted her hand in greeting, the woman dropped the scarf from her face, and Shaina looked straight into the eyes of her mother. With a scream of delight, she threw herself into Ona's outstretched arms, and their tears mingled. When, at last, they could speak, Shaina introduced Navit to her grandmother. Ona took a long look at the girl and sighed.

"Oh, that Nathan could see you, child. For you are everything I was when he found me selling silks in the marketplace those hundreds of years ago. Come to me, dear one." She took Navit's face between her hands and gazed into the clear, green eyes. "God has granted my wish to see you. Now I can die in peace."

"Don't speak of dying, Mother," Shaina interjected, leading her horse up the hillside. "We will have many years of happiness together here in this safe retreat."

Ira had moved, years before, onto the valley floor, saying his tired, old legs rebelled at the hillside. So the stone house had become Adriel and Shaina's, even though they often preferred the cave with its hawk's-eye view of the valley. It was there they took Ona now, and as Shaina prepared food, they talked furiously, their words leapfrogging and overlapping in their need to cover hundreds of years of living.

"Are you sure you can be happy in this place? It's very quiet here," Shaina worried, thinking of her mother's love for crowds and dancing.

Ona and Adriel exchanged glances, and Ona replied, some of the old mischief lighting her eyes, "I am a new person, with new desires, my daughter. After your father was killed, I was angry with his God, but also, deep inside, I respected Nathan for at last having the courage of his convictions.

"Ben was kind to me and built a small house for me at the back of his property, and with the money I had was able to live comfortably. But as the years passed, watched him change from the fine young man who had come to us from Havilah, to a cruel, scheming, pleasure mad tyrant. I had to admit that the farther he got from his beginnings, the more degraded he became. So I guess in the end, it was Abigail's long arm that reached out and touched me. I tried to recall how you and Ira had lived and I did my best to follow God in my ignorant way.

"When I heard there was a preacher of God at the marketplace, I went to have a look, and there, to my astonishment, was Adriel."

"It didn't take me long to persuade her to come with us," Shaina's husband grinned, still delighted at his surprise.

"Oh, Mother," Shaina murmured, taking the older woman's hand in hers. "All these years I've treasured the blue comb and my memory of you waving goodbye on that long-ago morning. I never dared to hope I would see you again. And here you are, not just your dear old self but a new self who shares our love for God. I wish I could tell Enoch. He would be so pleased."

"I expect he knows," Adriel reminded her, stretching out on the fur rug with his head in her lap. "Oh, my love it's good to be home."

"What did Ben say about all this?" Shaina asked, still trying to absorb the miracle of her mother's presence.

"He said, 'Get out and never let me see your faces again. I am no longer your kinsman, but your enemy. Remember that!' " A sadness tinged Adriel's voice at the memory.

"He's no longer the Ben you loved, Shaina," Ona added. "Sometimes, after I became a follower of God, I was very frightened of him."

They spoke no more of Ben, each mourning one they had loved.

Shaina never lost the wonder of her mother's faithfulness to her newfound God. She was still Ona, merry and nimble of tongue, but beneath the lighthearted exterior was a bedrock of solid commitment.

"I just can't wait," Shaina said to Navit one day, "until the Promised One calls us all from our graves and I bring Mother by the hand to my father. Just to see the look on his face. To have his beloved for all eternity."

"Don't rush us all into the grave, Mother," Navit cautioned, "though I'm eager to share in that moment myself. She's brought something special to the valley, sort of a renewed hope and a happy outlook on life."

"She's always been special." Shaina shaded her eyes and gazed along the valley toward the north. There a lone rider picked his way among the cliffs. "Run to the sheep pasture and tell your father a stranger approaches from the north." Shaina was already scrambling down the hillside toward Methuselah's dwelling so fast that small rocks and pebbles rattled about her leather sandals. By the time the visitor had entered the valley, Adriel and Methuselah stood resolutely in his path, backed by most of the valley residents.

"Peace," he hailed them, his white teeth flashing in his sun-bronzed face. "I am Noah, son of Lamech, grandson of Methuselah." [2]

With a glad cry Methuselah, his wife, Jonine, and Rimona rushed to embrace him, a grandson unseen since childhood.

"What brings you, son?" Methuselah asked, walking beside the horse, beaming with pleasure.

"Father sent me to determine the welfare of our kinsmen here in the valley and for other reasons," he informed them, grinning boyishly, though well into manhood.

The arrival of a guest excited the entire valley, and the women prepared a special meal for the evening. Before they ate, they all bowed about the outdoor tables, and

Methuselah prayed to the God of heaven, thanking Him for Noah's safe arrival and inviting His presence into their celebration. As dusk fell over the soft summer night, the people lighted oil-filled pots, and with the stars bright above their heads, they welcomed Noah great-grandson of Enoch, with singing and fellowship. When the older ones began to tire, Rimona called to Navit at a table some distance away, "Sing us a song child, for the journey home."

So with her father's flute as a soft accompaniment, Navit stood on one of the tables and sang an ancient tune of praise which old Amos had taught her as a child. It was a triumphant song, full of courage and hope in the Promised One, and as the valley dwellers followed various pathways homeward, the clear lilting voice unfurled over the velvet night like the banner of God. Noah turned to glance back and drew in his breath at the beauty of the slim, dark-haired girl amongst the flickering pots.

Lamech's son settled into the valley routine with no apparent urgency to leave. He traveled once with Adrie and his grandfather to preach in the cities, and they missed him in the valley. Although easy to know and quick to sense another's need, he was not a jovial man Noah had a quietness about him that some found restful, others intriguing, a few annoying, and all sobering.

Once Navit, carrying grain to the sheep pasture chanced upon him guarding the flock. Before he sensed her presence, she had opportunity to observe his strong angular face beneath its shock of unruly black hair. *A most unusual man,* she thought.

Becoming aware of her, he turned and smiled, that quick, dazzling smile that so fleetingly lit his sober face. "I feel rather useless sitting here in the sunshine all day waiting for a wolf to creep up on the sheep," he confessed shyly.

He's not comfortable with women, Navit concluded, especially a young woman all alone in a flowered meadow. "Well, it's a pleasant way to spend the day, so don't waste it by feeling guilty," she advised, pouring the grain into a long hollowed trough, fending off the crowding sheep with one knee. "What would you be doing if you were home?"

"We work with leather, making sandals and tunics and many other items. My father learned the trade here as a boy from our grandmother, Rimona. As often as possible we travel from one city to another with the message of the Promised One, as does your father. We sell the leather goods, and it provides us entrance into the cities, as they value our product and will thus put up with our preaching."

Navit, pushing her dark hair away from her perspiring face, slipped into the shade of the large rock upon which Noah sat. "I often wonder if our existence here has any purpose. We live this simple, pastoral life while the world passes us by. What good are we to God?"

Noah studied the young face before him and thought he had never seen such innocence and purity. "You are guarding a way of life that is fast fading," he assured her. "Beyond this valley, men who were once valiant for God now serve Him in word only. They no longer observe seventh day as sacred, and their gardens gleam with idols. It is hard to remain pure in a world permeated with sin and rebellion. But here, Navit, here in the simplicity of nature, people live as God meant them to. There's a spirit of praise and prayer ever rising, and one feels close to the Creator."

"I am content here," she said. She paused a moment. "Don't your wife and children miss you while you are with us?"

"Not at all," he answered gravely, a hint of amusement in his black eyes. He was quiet a moment, enjoying her puzzled expression. "You see, I have not married."

It was Navit's turn to be shy. Suddenly she felt very young and unsure before this man who had seen the world and graced her valley briefly with his presence. Dropping her gaze, she felt the color flooding her cheeks and had no idea why it was happening.

Noah continued calmly. "Though I have looked about a bit, I never found a woman who was really God's person, at least not one who pleased me. I preferred loneliness rather than compromise, so here I am, more than 300 years old and alone in the world. I am rather used to it by now, but my father insisted I come here to search for a true woman of God."

"Well, it was a poor idea," Navit said frankly. "There are only a handful of young women here, and none your age."

"So I have found," he admitted humbly.

It wasn't her nature to be rude, and Navit could not imagine why she had spoken so sharply. "I must be going," she called over her shoulder as she gathered her empty grain sacks and headed toward home.

"I shall feel useless again if you leave," he answered good-naturedly, but she did not turn or look back. Nor, strangely enough, did she speak of the conversation with her parents at the evening meal.

She made it a point to avoid Noah after that, and wished she'd never discovered he had no wife. What did it matter? How did it change anything? He was an honorable man, and she only a child in his sight, no doubt. But nevertheless, she kept out of his way.

A few weeks later Methuselah climbed the hillside to the cave in the late afternoon. Behind him Jonine and Rimona came bearing bowls of steaming food and baked delicacies. "We would have you break bread with us, Adriel," Methuselah announced. "We have an important matter to discuss."

Soon Ira and Ona also came puffing up the steep bank, and Shaina realized the matter of discussion must ndeed be a grave one. Adriel's face was impassive and he found no answer there. They shared the food, speaking of trivial matters, but the atmosphere was subdued. Finally Ona, caring little for tradition, spoke up. "How long must we wait to hear your message, Methuselah? These fine foods are wasted in the tension of the moment, and I for one would like to enjoy them."

Navit smothered a smile. Leave it to her grandmother to break through the aura of reserve that surrounded the patriarch. Methuselah glanced uneasily at his wife. Navit had never seen him less than confident before, and her curiosity grew. Finally he turned to Rimona.

"You are better at such things than I, my mother. Would you . . . ?" he faltered uncomfortably.

Smiling, Rimona shook her head in maternal amusement at her tall, weathered son, but Navit noted that she too did not seem totally at ease. "My dear ones"—she looked about at the little group eating grapes and spitting seeds over the lip of the cliff—"what we come to request tonight is not being handled in the custom of our ancestors, but it is an unusual situation. Our grandson Noah, whom you all know, did not come to this valley simply to herd sheep and visit his relatives. He seeks a mate who is pure before God."

Has he chosen someone? Navit thought, her mind racing wildly over the few eligible young women of the valley. She had seen him with none of them, but then, she had avoided him.

"Two days ago," Rimona continued, "he told us he had found the woman who made all his years of waiting worthwhile." Shaina saw the color drain from Adriel's face. "To our utter astonishment, he said it was Navit." Rimona looked at Shaina, her beloved friend of many years, hoping that she would understand.

No one said a word for several moments, and Navit felt her heart pounding in her chest. She wondered if the rest could hear it. Adriel spoke at last, his voice firm.

"We are honored, but she is far too young, my friends, t⸱ leave the valley."

Navit sat with downcast eyes, feeling somehow beret at her father's finality. He was right, of course, so why was she experiencing a sense of dull disappointment?

"I will accept your decision, of course, my husband but I would remind you of a day long ago when I joine you in coming to this valley, and my father refused hi permission. My mother intervened." Shaina glanced a Ona and smiled. "I have always been grateful for he understanding, and I have never regretted my decisio⸱ Maybe we need to ask Navit how she feels about thi matter."

With all eyes upon her, the young woman struggle for composure. She felt herself bombarded with emo tions. Fear, confusion, amazement, and somethin else—a small flame of joy, which she tried unsuccess fully to squelch. "I cannot say so suddenly." Tear threatened to come. "I would like time to think and pray and I would also like to talk to Noah."

"That is not the custom." Adriel's glance defied her t stand against his paternal judgment. He had not antic pated the slightest interest on his daughter's part.

Rimona reminded him quietly, "It's very hard to follo⸱ tradition here in the valley, Adriel. How traditional wa your marriage to Shaina? Who arranged it? Is it not bett⸱ if Noah and Navit talk together about their feelings an their future? Perhaps they will decide it is not a practic⸱ union after all."

Practical! Navit thought, laughing nervously to herse⸱ Whatever she felt for Noah, it had nothing to do wit being practical. It felt free and beautiful like a butterfl and as hard to capture. Although it was so ethereal tha her mind could not get hold of it, her heart had knowr she admitted ruefully, since the day in the sheep pa⸱ ture.

When Noah climbed, the next afternoon, up to th⸱

cave, Shaina busied herself with her clay and suggested that Noah and Navit go through the tunnel into the place of prayer for privacy. Noah had never seen the sunlit nook, and he gasped at its beauty. Shaina had filled pockets in the surrounding cliff with soil, and tiny bell-shaped coral flowers now tumbled airily from the rock wall. A small rivulet splashed into a pool, and the pungent odor of mint hung in the warm air.

Why had she insisted upon talking with him? Navit thought in panic. *What would she say now that he was here? Had they really expected her just to ride away with a man to whom she had spoken only a few words? Why didn't he say something?*

Noah stood, quietly looking down at her, waiting.

What was he waiting for? If he wanted her in mar-riage, then let him say so. Let him *speak first. If he was such a strange, stubborn creature, perhaps it was best to find it out now.*

So they faced each other there in the enclosed garden, the sun warm on their heads. After a while the irritation drained from her and she felt a kind of peace, just being there with him in the stillness.

Only then did he speak. "Navit, my beautiful one." He touched her soft, dark cloud of hair gently, wonderingly. "Let us kneel here in this place and seek God's counsel." He prayed then such a prayer as she had never heard before. A prayer full of his love for her, his longing to take her forever into his home and heart, but a prayer also of complete submission to the will of God. "And if she goes with me, Lord, I vow to care for her tenderly all the days of my life, but if she chooses to stay here in the valley, I shall accept it as Your holy sign that I am to work for You alone forever, for I could never love another."

Then he lapsed into silence, though he remained upon his knees, head bowed, lips still moving in prayer.

Navit reached out and gently brushed her finger tips

against his mouth. "Enough. Enough, my beloved. God has heard and answered. I am little more than a child, but I will go with you, and together we will do His will and His work."

Noah looked at her then, his black eyes glistening with tears. He did not touch her, but in his glance she saw more promise than she had ever dreamed existed.

* * * * *

When the marrying and the celebrating were done, the two prepared to leave the valley. For the first time Shaina understood what her parents had endured long years before when she too rode away, never to return. While she and Adriel agonized, it was Ona who assured them of the great reunion when the Promised One would make all things new.[3]

The three stood together, smiling through their tears, as Noah and Navit mounted their steeds and led two packhorses toward the rocky path through which Noah had entered the valley. In Navit's hair, Nathan's blue comb held her soft curls back from her face. Shaina had placed it there herself, lovingly, saying, "Someday, my darling, perhaps you too shall have a daughter, and you will tell her of the love between your grandmother and her potter husband. And you will tell her how he died at the hands of a mob for his God. And then you will place this comb in her hair, as I am placing it in yours. We are the women of Havilah, Navit, daughters of Abigail. Never forget it. Though that valley is lost to us, the heritage is not. It is for us to hold the name of God high above the evil of this world. You are going beyond the safe walls of this valley where you were born. For the first time you will see evil in all its bold defiance of the God of heaven. Fight against it as Enoch did, by walking closely with God, and then share with others the knowledge of the God you have come to know and love."

Shaina had wept then, gathering her daughter into her

arms, thinking that 22 years was not nearly enough time in which to treasure one's only child. This man, Noah. Was he fine enough for her innocent, clear-eyed daughter, who had graced the valley with her laughter and her love and her songs? She hoped so. "Oh, my child," she'd whispered, drying her eyes at last, "I love you so. God go with you."

And now they were only specks climbing upward toward the skyline, and she felt Adriel's grief as he held her. He's lost so much, all his life, she realized. Both of his daughters. She would devote herself to his happiness. Slowly she turned him then toward home and dried his tears with her own hands. "Come, my love. Navit goes strong in the blood of our people. We have given her to God. Let us not do it with mourning."

She darted away from him, running, teasing, looking over her shoulder, laughing. She was once more the girl he'd brought through the dark forests to this valley, and he ran after her, catching her up, breathless, in his arms, and they tried to smile again, little dreaming the destiny toward which Navit rode beside her sober, godly husband.

* * * * *

Shaina, having arisen early to talk with God and to watch the sunrise, sat on the rim of rock overhanging the valley, lost in meditation. The soft peach of morning spilled over into the valley, and it was then she saw them, slipping one by one through the slot in the rock, hardly more than shadows in the early dawn. Scrambling to her feet, she ran to the corner where Adriel still slept and shook him roughly.

"Wake up, love. There are people entering the valley—lots of them. Hurry."

Adriel slipped into his clothes, and together they watched an endless line of riders flow down the far slope. He turned toward his wife, his face sad. "My beautiful Shaina, our life together here in the valley is over. We shall die as our people died, strong in the Lord. Be brave."

They woke Ona, sleeping in the stone house, and together the three walked to the valley floor where with ominous quiet the intruders already crept from home to home, doing their deadly work upon the sleeping victims.

Adriel advanced to meet the mounted leader seated tall upon his horse, bright ribbons on the harness flapping smartly in the morning breeze. In the semidarkness Shaina, following behind him, strained to see the man's face, and when she came close enough, she let out a little cry of horror, for it was the same face that she had once loved. But it was hardened now with age and evil. Behind Ben rode Tobias, obviously in a position of honor, and she realized that what Methuselah had long feared had happened. As civilization crept close on all sides, one who knew the secret entrance to the valley had, for a price, revealed all.

As though in a trance, she heard Adriel's calm voice speaking. "Ben, what betrayal of all we shared as kinsmen brings you to this moment?"

The man from Havilah looked down at the three of them as though at strangers. Shaina grew faint at the cries rising from all over the valley as armed men slaughtered the worshipers of God. Ben addressed her husband, and his words were cold with hatred. "You took them all from me, Adriel, one by one. After you left, Nathan was never again content in the city. He hungered for the old Havilah ways and the worship of God. I lost him long before he died, because of you.

"You took Shaina, the only woman I ever loved, and dragged her to this forsaken spot, but that was not enough. You took her as your wife, she who was my betrothed. And even that was not enough, Adriel. You came back and carried Ona away, the last that I had.

Don't speak to me of betrayal."

Ona fearlessly approached and looked up at the man she had taken into her home those many years ago. "Ben," she said, her voice amazingly controlled, almost gentle, "you know that is not the truth. All of us turned willingly to God. Adriel had nothing to do with it. He begged you to go with them when he and Shaina left that early morning. You cannot blame this slaughter upon him. It is the power of the evil one dwelling in you that brought you to this place. You were like a son to me for many years. How could you do this thing?"

Ben spoke but a word, and his men fell upon her, and then Adriel. Shaina stood like stone, waiting for the blow to fall, but Ben reined his horse between her and the spears and said sharply, "She will live. See that no harm comes to her.

"Go to your cave," he ordered her, "and may your pain be as mine has been." He watched her climb the hill, the first sunlight catching her shining hair.

* * * * *

They never bothered her, the newcomers, as they constructed their small city, and the years rolled on. Nor did they venture near her stone house. A portion of every harvest was left upon her doorstep, and by selling her clay creations in the public market, she managed to survive. Now and then she met Ben upon some well-worn path, but he never spoke, averting his gaze as if she were a stranger. She attempted to become friends with the women, hoping to speak to them of the true God, or at least to assuage her loneliness, but they recoiled from her, uncomfortable, and she knew some invisible mark had been placed upon her—that in the end, Ben's gift of life was worse than a speedy death and that he had planned it that way.

There were only her and her God, and in the hidden place of prayer she drew closer and closer to Him until the loneliness at last became peace, and then joy.

Sometimes in the darkness of sixth night the city dwellers heard her singing the ancient songs of God's people, and now and then hearts trembled with memories of Enoch's words and forebodings for the future.

.

[1] "According to the Lord's own word, we tell you that we who are still alive, who are left till the coming of the Lord, will certainly not precede those who have fallen asleep. For the Lord Himself will come down from heaven, with a loud command, with the voice of the archangel and with the trumpet call of God, and the dead in Christ will rise first" (1 Thessalonians 4:15, 16).

[2] "When Methuselah had lived 187 years, he became the father of Lamech. . . . When Lamech had lived 182 years, he had a son. He named him Noah and said, 'He will comfort us in the labor and painful toil of our hands caused by the ground the Lord has cursed' " (Genesis 5:25-29).

[3] "Do not let your hearts be troubled. Trust in God; trust also in me. In my Father's house are many rooms; if it were not so, I would have told you. I am going there to prepare a place for you. And if I go and prepare a place for you, I will come back and take you to be with me that you also may be where I am" (John 14:1-3).

"Behold, I will create new heavens and a new earth. The former things will not be remembered, nor will they come to mind" (Isaiah 65:17).

" 'They will build houses and dwell in them; they will plant vineyards and eat their fruit. No longer will they build houses and others live in them, or plant and others eat. For as the days of a tree, so will be the days of my people; my chosen ones will long enjoy the works of their hands. They will not toil in vain or bear children doomed to misfortune; for they will be a people blessed by the LORD, they and their descendants with them. Before they call I will answer; while they are still speaking I will hear. The wolf and the lamb will feed together, and the lion will eat straw like the ox, but dust will be the serpent's food. They will neither harm nor destroy on all my holy mountain,' says the LORD" (Isaiah 65:21-25).

"But in keeping with his promise we are looking forward to

a new heaven and a new earth, the home of righteousness" (2 Peter 3:13).

"And the ransomed of the LORD will return. They will enter Zion with singing; everlasting joy will crown their heads. Gladness and joy will overtake them, and sorrow and sighing will flee away" (Isaiah 35:10).

"And without faith it is impossible to please God, because anyone who comes to him must believe that he exists and that he rewards those who earnestly seek him" (Hebrews 11:6).

" 'As the new heavens and the new earth that I make will endure before me,' declares the LORD, 'so will your name and descendants endure. From one New Moon to another and from one Sabbath to another, all mankind will come and bow down before me,' says the LORD" (Isaiah 66:22, 23).

"Then I saw a new heaven and a new earth, for the first heaven and the first earth had passed away, and there was no longer any sea. I saw the Holy City, the new Jerusalem, coming down out of heaven from God, prepared as a bride beautifully dressed for her husband. And I heard a loud voice from the throne saying, 'Now the dwelling of God is with men, and he will live with them. They will be his people, and God himself will be with them and be their God. He will wipe every tear from their eyes. There will be no more death or mourning or crying or pain, for the old order of things has passed away.' He who was seated on the throne said, 'I am making everything new!' Then he said, 'Write this down, for these words are trustworthy and true.' He said to me: 'It is done. I am the Alpha and the Omega, the Beginning and the End. To him who is thirsty I will give to drink without cost from the spring of the water of life. He who overcomes will inherit all this, and I will be his God and he will be my son. But the cowardly, the unbelieving, the vile, the murderers, the sexually immoral, those who practice magic arts, the idolaters and all liars—their place will be in the fiery lake of burning sulfur. This is the second death.' One of the seven angels who had the seven bowls full of the seven last plagues came and said to me, 'Come, I will show you the bride, the wife of the Lamb.' And he carried me away in the Spirit to a mountain great and high, and showed me the Holy City, Jerusalem, coming down out of heaven from God. It shone with the glory of God, and its brilliance was like that of a very precious jewel, like a jasper, clear as crystal. It had a great, high wall with twelve gates, and with twelve angels at the gates. On the gates were written the names of the twelve tribes of Israel. There were three gates on the east, three on the north, three on the south and three on the west. The wall of the city had twelve foundations, and on them were the names of the twelve apostles of the Lamb. The angel who talked with me had a measuring rod of gold to measure the city, its gates and its walls. The city was laid out like a square, as long as it was wide. He measured the city with the rod and found it to be 12,000 stadia in length, and as wide and high as it is long. He measured its wall and it was 144 cubits. thick, by man's measurement, which the angel was using. The wall was made of jasper, and the city of pure gold, as pure as glass. The foundations of the city walls were decorated with every kind of precious stone. The first foundation was jasper, the second sapphire, the third chalcedony, the fourth emerald, the fifth sardonyx, the sixth carnelian, the seventh chrysolite, the eighth beryl, the ninth topaz, the tenth chrysoprase, the eleventh jacinth, and the twelfth amethyst. The twelve gates were twelve pearls, each gate made of a single pearl. The great street of the city was of pure gold, like transparent glass. I did not see a temple in the city, because the Lord God Almighty and the Lamb are its temple. The city does not need the sun or the moon to shine on it, for the glory of God gives it light, and the Lamb is its lamp. The nations will walk by its light, and the kings of the earth will bring their splendor into it. On no day will its gates ever be shut, for there will be no night there. The glory and honor of the nations will be brought into it. Nothing impure will ever enter it, nor will anyone who does what is shameful or deceitful, but only those whose names are written in the Lamb's book of life" (Revelation 21).

"Then the angel showed me the river of the water of life, as clear as crystal, flowing from the throne of God and of the Lamb down the middle of the great street of the city. On each side of the river stood the tree of life, bearing twelve crops of fruit, yielding its fruit every month. And the leaves of the tree are for the healing of the nations. No longer will there be any curse. The throne of God and of the Lamb will be in the city, and his servants will serve him. They will see his face, and his name will be on their foreheads. There will be no more night. They will not need the light of a lamp or the light of the sun for the Lord God will give them light. And they will reign for ever and ever. The angel said to me, 'These words are trustworthy and true. The Lord, the God of the spirits of the prophets, sent his angel to show his servants the things that must soon take place.' 'Behold, I am coming soon! Blessed is he who keeps the words of the prophecy in this book.' I, John, am the one who heard and saw these things. And when I had heard and seen them, I fell down to worship at the feet of the angel who had been showing them to me. But he said to me, 'Do not do it! I am a fellow servant with you and with your brothers the prophets and of all who keep the words of this book. Worship God!' Then he told me, 'Do not seal up the words of the prophecy of this book, because the time is near. Let him who does wrong continue to do wrong; let him who is vile continue to be vile; let him who does right continue to do right; and let him who is holy continue to be holy. Behold, I am coming soon! My reward is with me, and I will give to everyone according to what he has done. I am the Alpha and the Omega, the First and the Last, the Beginning and the End. Blessed are those who wash their robes, that they may have the right to the tree of life and may go through the gates into the city. Outside are the dogs, those who practice magic arts, the sexually immoral, the murderers, the idolaters and everyone who loves and practices falsehood. I, Jesus, have sent my angel to give you this testimony for the churches. I am the Root and the Offspring of David, and the bright Morning Star.' The Spirit and the bride say, 'Come!' And let him who hears say, 'Come!' Whoever is thirsty, let him come; and whoever wishes, let him take the free gift of the water of life. I warn everyone who hears the words of the prophecy of this book: If anyone adds anything to them, God will add to him the plagues described in this book. And If anyone takes words away from this book of prophecy, God will take away from him his share in the tree of life and in the holy city, which are described in this book. He who testifies to these things says, 'Yes, I am coming soon.' Amen. Come, Lord Jesus. The grace of the Lord Jesus be with God's people. Amen" (Revelation 22).

THE BOAT

Navit stood a moment, shaking crumbs from a table cover on the step of the long, low house of oak that Noah had built for her during the first years after their arrival in this place. The house tucked neatly into the angle of the hillside and seemed almost a part of the original creation, with its banks of flowers and shrubs tumbling away from it. Before her lay a great shallow bowl of green meadow, fragrant now with clover and dotted with the herds of Noah and their sons. The encircling horizon was a soft scallop of gently rolling hills. Small cities lay within a half day's journey, and some travelers came and went along an old route in their northwest grazing lands, but Noah was respected and his family lived life quite apart from the travelers who wended their way from one place to another.

Or at least that's how it had been until Noah began to build the boat.[1] Folding the cloth neatly, she turned to observe the scene, not far from the road, that was now filled with the curious, filled and overflowing into their once-quiet meadow.

Over a tremendous, nearly enclosed skeleton of cypress beams, men swarmed in a variety of tasks. Three of them were her sons, Shem, Ham, and Japheth. One was the old patriarch Methuselah, and there were many of Noah's uncles and cousins. She had about lost track of them all, especially since her husband had much hired help, also.

The construction site contained a number of buildings to house the workers, a large structure in which they ate, and lodgings in which travelers might stay and observe and listen to Noah's sometimes tender, sometimes severe appeals for their souls.

Their lives had changed greatly since that night Noah had come in from his evening time of prayer, his face ashen beneath sun-darkened skin. Calling Methuselah, who lived in their home, he had drawn Navit close to his side on a bench, and with the oil lamp casting long shadows across the golden wood of the walls, he told them that the angel of the Lord had approached him. They did not question his announcement, knowing that Noah walked in the holy footsteps of his great-grandfather Enoch.[2]

Obviously shaken, Noah had sat quietly for a few moments, attempting to collect himself. Navit stroked his arm lightly, and he calmed, as ever, at her touch.

Finally, he went on. "I was in prayer, but even with my eyes closed, I sensed a light so bright it pierced through me like a spear, and I fell flat upon the earth in terror." Navit remembered her mother's story of the light at Eden's gate.

"Have we sinned, Noah?" she asked, fear in her voice.

"We all sin,[3] dear one," Noah replied, "but that was not the message. The judgment that Enoch predicted is about to fall upon those who defy God and refuse to have faith in the Promised One." The magnitude of what he had experienced, the terrible message of doom for millions, pressed upon him, and he wept. "Oh, that someone else had been chosen for this awful task," he groaned.

Methuselah, gnarled and gray with age, spoke from his seat by the window. "It is not a small thing to have found favor in the eyes of God.[4] Take up your mission with trust in Him who called you, and let us warn all that we can."

"What are we to do?" Navit sensed there was more to her husband's story.

"We are to build a large boat," Noah mused, still stunned.

"A boat!" She laughed in spite of herself. "Dear one, there's no water larger than a lake or a stream for miles around. What are we to do with a boat?"

"There is going to be a flood,[5] Navit, which will cover the earth; and only those in the boat will be saved."

"Flood?" Methuselah eyed his grandson sharply. "Did the great God explain what a flood is?"

"The earth will be covered with water," Noah repeated patiently, "even above the tops of the mountains."

"And where will all this water come from?" the old man persisted.

Noah sighed. "From the heavens and from the depths of the earth. And do not ask me to explain that, for I cannot. I can tell you only what was told me. The angel used the term *rain* in speaking of water from the sky." [6]

Navit thought of the mist that fell over the earth each morning before dawn, gently watering every growing thing. *"Rain."* She tested the new word upon her tongue and tried to imagine water falling from that great, sunny, blue expanse that arched above them day by day.

"How will we accomplish such a feat?" The old one stretched his long legs wearily out before him.

"God laid out the plan carefully.[7] It will take all our time and all our money. Our leather business must go. God has given us 120 years in which to construct the vessel and warn the world. We will live from our gardens and our herds. But we will have to employ many laborers. In the end it could well take everything we own." He looked at Navit beside him, her olive skin touched with the glow of health, her dark hair curling loosely about her face. Her green eyes, clear and trusting, gazed back into his.

"It's all right, Noah," she whispered, a faint smile curving her lips. "Whatever God says, it's all right."

* * * * *

We've come a long way, she thought now, standing there in the sunlight on her doorstep. One hundred eighteen years of labor and ridicule. At first some had listened, sobered by Noah's message. They'd even helped with the work. But as the years rolled on, the craft and her husband became a joke. The people called him crazy, a fool. The crowds came to watch and taunt. Only on seventh day, when the family rested, did they know peace, and even then the curious brazenly wandered through the ark, marveling at the meticulous construction while they scoffed at Noah's message.

Right now Navit could hear the voice of her husband, lifted above the confusion of hammering and babble. Though she could not sort out the words, she knew them well. "Time is growing short, my friends. God will have an accounting. You have used the riches of the earth with no thought of obedience to the God who provides. You fall upon your knees before idols of silver and sacrifice your children upon altars of gold. You create your own gods to worship. But the true God, the Creator, you scorn. You refuse to have faith in the Promised One. You have no sorrow for your sins, and doom lies at your door.[8]

"Water will cover the earth. Only those who enter the boat will be safe. You have caused God to regret His creation. Turn, turn now, from your evil ways while there is time. God is merciful. God forgives."

She had heard him a thousand times and no longer listened to their shouts of derision.

"Shall we all bring a jug of water on the big day, Noah?"

"Too much sun has gone to your head, Noah."

"What makes you think you are so much holier than we, Noah?"

Now and then she'd see someone on the edge of the crowd really listening, and she'd go and stand with him, urging him to take seriously Noah's words. "It isn't much God is asking. Just to go inside when Noah calls you. Just to trust His words. Listen to my husband. He is a man of God. He would not lie to you." She never knew whether it helped or not, but she kept on trying.

And her sons. She was proud of them. They went on hammering, sawing, and applying pitch through it all. On that night when Noah had revealed his message from the Lord, he had told Navit later, in the privacy of their bed, that in the covenant God had made with him,[9] He'd mentioned sons and even their wives. "I didn't feel it necessary to remind the Creator that we had no sons," he'd added, chuckling.

"It means I will bear children, my darling," Navit breathed in such an ecstasy of joy that her husband laughed again and drew her to him.

"I expect that's exactly what He meant," he murmured into the softness of her dark hair. "The fields of Noah shall be filled with the laughter of little ones and the felling of trees. Oh, my sweet girl, the years ahead are solemn ones, but *sons, can you imagine, Navit, sons?*"

Hearing the exultation in his voice, she realized the intense longing that had been his during the barren years. He'd hidden it to spare her, but now, now that the promise was sure, he could let it all out in a wild rejoicing that she felt in every fiber of his lean muscular frame. She drank of his excitement, and they clung together, laughing and crying, longing for the fulfillment of fertility.

But it had been 20 years before the birth of Japheth.[10] Sometimes during that period Navit had wondered if he had even heard God correctly, but her husband never doubted. At the first indication of her motherhood, he built a new altar and made a sacrifice of thanksgiving. The sons had come then, three of them, one quickly upon the other, until it seemed to Navit she had always walked with her back arched and her belly rolling out like a plump melon before her. But she had loved every moment of it. The movement of life within her, the strong maternal urges that swept over her, the ripe swelling of her body as she nurtured the seed of Noah. All too quickly it was over, and she regained her slim figure soon enough chasing three little boys about, keeping them away from the crowds and out of the way of the builders.

In the evenings Noah took them through the structure, explaining the work, the purpose, the sacred assignment. There in the awesome spreading framework he taught them to bend their little knees before God and to lisp simple prayers after him. They grew into strong, towering, young men, one sandy like his Havilah forefathers, the other two dark and brooding like their father. *And they knew nothing but the boat.* They knew the noise of great trees thundering down with a crash that shook the earth for miles around. They knew the struggle to cut the beautiful wood, hard as stone. They knew the driving perfection of their father's will as he built according to holy plan. They knew blazing sun on their dark backs, calluses on their hands, and the rhythm of hammers unceasingly in their ears.

Navit worried that their wives would not remain faithful to the mission. Noah had found for his sons distant cousins, descendants of Enoch, carefully chosen, but the young women had already acquired many worldly ways before they became a part of Noah's household. Tactfully, lovingly, Navit spoke to them of the true God, but she thought in the end that it was Noah's humble integrity that won them.

Her father-in-law, Lamech, had died three years earlier, but Methuselah labored on. Navit loved having him with them, for he alone had shared the old days in Enoch's valley. They spoke often of those gentler times, and of Rimona, Jonine, Shaina, and Adriel. Methuselah had been gone from the valley when Ben's invasion brought death to all but Shaina. When he returned and saw the muddy trampling of earth about the entrance, he had guessed at once the catastrophe that had befallen its inhabitants. Cautiously he circled the valley until, at the north end, he had been able to view the length of it and saw, as he had expected, the frenzy of building taking place. Recognizing no one, he had assumed all to be dead, and in deep sorrow he set out to find his son Lamech and grandson Noah. He and Navit had been drawn close in their mutual mourning, and he moved gladly into her home, healing gradually under her care.

After the birth of her sons, Navit longed achingly for her mother. Today she yearned to show Shaina the fragrant meadow with its strange structure rearing at one end. She longed to point out the three brown figures who were her sons, to boast a bit of their faithfulness to the task and to God. And she wanted her mother to know of the love between her and Noah, the wild, sweet love that knit them forever together. She'd seen the doubts in her parents' eyes when she and Noah had ridden away. Now she wanted them to know that it had been right— more right than she could have dreamed—to give herself to Noah. That in all the pressures of his work for God, he never failed to come to her in the evening for comfort and nurture, and to show her the most tender affection. It was as though the wonder of his finding her had never waned and the fresh discovery of her upon his hearth, day by day, filled him with amazing joy. If only her mother could know that!

Shem's wife, Zoe, called to her from the sheep pens, and Navit ran to the wooden fence that rambled across the east section of their land. "Could you bring us something to drink, Mother?" the tall girl requested from where she held a sheep pinned between her knees as she expertly sheared the struggling animal. Zoe had gradually assumed the responsibility of the cattle and sheep as the men's construction work demanded more and more time. Navit marveled at her strong, lean look as she wrestled another sheep into submission. The herds and flocks had thrived under her care, providing the family with clothing and food. Navit and the other two, Malka and Nasya, cared for the crops and gardens. They had labored like men, but the work had released a glowing vitality in them until Noah and his sons marveled at their beauty. The eight of them were as one, preaching, building, storing, a single concentrated unit to prepare a people and a place for the time of rain.

Navit hurried toward the house to bring refreshment to Zoe and her shearers.

That evening, as Noah told them of the tremendous quantities of food that they must now begin to place in the boat for both man and beast,[11] Methuselah seemed detached, far removed from them somehow. Noah often depended on the old man's magnificent memory, and he spoke to him now with a hint of impatience. "Grandfather, I want you in charge of supplying the boat. I must transfer these figures from my mind to yours, so that I need not spend the time involved in gathering grains and dried fruits. There will be no strenuous work involved for you. Leave that to younger backs than yours. But I need your dependable mind to supervise."

Methuselah looked at his grandson fondly. They had conducted the work of God many years together through severe dangers and small victories. "My son," he said lovingly, "you will have to store your counsel in some other mind, for I am going on a last journey from which I shall not return."

Navit gasped. Was he talking of death? She could see him struggling up the path to the cave, those many years ago, bearing food and later searching for words to plead Noah's love for her. What was he talking about now, here in this place that had become home to him?

"I'm going to make a last visit to the cities and warn them of the rains," he continued. "Thousands have heard only rumors. They will remember me. They will know I speak truth. Perhaps a few will heed the warning. Should my life be spared, I shall go, at the last, to Father's valley and surely there meet my death, but perhaps not before I have had my say and given them a last opportunity."

He's speaking of those who murdered his beloved Jonine and his mother, Navit thought, her eyes filling with tears.

Noah started to speak, but Methuselah raised his hand. "Don't try to dissuade me, son. It is the will of God."

The next morning the old man rode out of sight along the route already filled with the curious and the mockers. Through their tears Navit and Noah watched him go, a giant, gentle, white-haired figure riding calmly toward sure death on his divine mission. "I wanted him on the boat with us," Navit wept, clinging to Noah.

Her husband sighed, gently rubbing his beard against her cheek. "I feel more alone than I believed possible. He was a great comfort and strength to me when they laughed and pelted me with their spoiled fruits."

"Now God will be your strength, my love," she said slowly. "Perhaps that's part of the plan." But after that, she stole time from her work as often as possible to stand beside him an hour when he spoke, letting the taunts and the missiles fall upon her, too, until she knew his pain in every corner of her being; and their love for each other and their God grew even more.

Shem, Ham, and Japheth worked with a single-minded intensity, sometimes far into the night when moonlight flooded the meadow, for the hired laborers grew few as disdain for the project peaked. Zoe, Malka, and Nasya, with Navit ever helping and encouraging, filled the great storage bins higher and higher with their grains and beans and sweet dried meadow grasses for the animals. The last months they worked almost alone, the seven, as Noah preached with a rising fervor.

* * * * *

Methuselah entered the valley from the rocky north end, picking his way along a seldom-used path. In a score of cities he had told the story of the great waters covering the earth. He barely escaped with his life from most of them. His heart ached with the things he had seen. The disease of sin and rebellion festered, malignant, upon the beautiful land, and humanity abused the precious gift of life in every conceivable way. Men fought over the fruitful places of earth, their blood soaking the green meadows and hidden valleys. Everywhere images rose from exquisite gardens, their benign faces belying their cruel demands. Methuselah longed for the quiet home of Noah and Navit, for the gentle fields where a great boat loomed into the sky, but he had one last mission here in his childhood home, and he did not expect to survive it.

For a moment he stood, scanning the length of the valley, remembering. He saw Navit, a little girl with dancing green eyes and bobbing black curls, trotting behind Shaina, carrying a basket of food for some ill or elderly one. His eyes wandered over the hillsides, bright with color, which Shaina and Ira had landscaped hundreds of years before. There wasn't much to recognize. The humble homes of God's people had all vanished, now replaced with structures so magnificent that the old man stared in wonder.

Slowly he made his way down toward the public market, and leaning his tired back against a pillar, warm with sun, he began to speak. Gradually the street traffic slowed and gathered about him, listening, laughing, calling out a taunt from time to time.

"My brothers," he said, his majestic old head turning from side to side, his eyes blazing into them. "I am

Methuselah. I grew up in this valley." A murmur rippled over the crowd. "My father, Enoch, whom God took, traveled from city to city warning of a judgment to come. Some of you remember him, I'm sure. He begged you to turn back to God. The hour of which he spoke is upon us."

Suddenly he caught a glimpse of a face that he had never dreamed to see again. Shaina stood before him in the crowd, her beautiful face aged but serene as an angel's. Her green eyes crinkled, smiling, as they met his, and she read his shock and delight. They made no sign of recognition, not daring, but their eyes clung, their joy almost tangible.

His voice trembling, Methuselah went on, speaking to the people, but also to Shaina—telling her all he dared.

"My grandson, Noah, builds a great boat in his field, a craft that will save the righteous when the waters fall from heaven and gush from the earth. He and his three sons have labored for 120 years. Any day now, God will cover the earth with water. None shall escape but those in the boat. It is the word of God. Go. Go now, while there is time. Believe the warning of the Lord. Find safety in the boat. Forsake your sins . . ."

At the word *sins,* a rumble of anger rose from the people, and they surged in a seething mass toward the old man. He heard Shaina's cry and felt her body hurled against him, shielding him, as they went down together beneath the weight of strong men and flailing fists. Before blackness took them, Shaina breathed a question, "Navit?"

And Methuselah answered, "Happy and well."

Ben buried them in Shaina's hidden place of prayer, where Adam's daffodils still bloomed. Then he had strong men roll a tremendous boulder into the mouth of the tunnel, sealing it forever, and went down the hillside, the taste of approaching doom bitter in his mouth.

* * * * *

Navit stood quietly beside Noah as he preached, her mind racing over lists of supplies, her eyes drifting across the indifferent faces before her. Soon she must prepare the noon meal, but she knew her husband drew strength from her presence, so she lingered on. Sometimes Shem replaced him for a few hours, and Navit was proud of her stalwart son as his steady voice rose above the jeers of the onlookers. She thought often of Methuselah, knowing some evil had befallen him to keep him so long away. The hope that he would enter the vessel with them died hard. Would it be only eight? Had 120 years of warning produced not one believer? Had Noah's voice been lifted in vain those thousands of times?

A small city had grown up around them. At first, just opportunists catering to the needs of the crowds; but others followed, drawn by the beauty of the place and the excitement ever present there. Golden images reared into the sky, and the sounds of drunken feasting shattered the stillness of their nights. Few listened anymore. Noah and his huge craft were tolerated simply as familiar amusements.

Navit had just started to slip away from her husband when she heard the strange noise and noted a sudden shadowing of the sunny meadow. Her gaze flew to the sky, and in astonishment she saw birds, thousands of them, drifting in a dark wave toward the boat, the beating of their wings like the roar of strong winds. "Noah," she breathed, "look what is happening."

He stopped in midsentence and scanned the heavens. "The word of God is being fulfilled. Surely now they will believe."

A great silence fell over the meadow, until one could only hear the beating of wings, and then, in the distance, the steady tread of beasts of every kind.[12]

They gathered on the ramp of the boat, Noah and his family, and watched the animals approach. Bears, tigers, elephants, leopards, geese, cows, horses, camels, tiny field mice, squirrels, foxes, giraffes. Animals they had never seen—domestic animals, wild beasts. They came in perfect order. Often Navit had wondered how they would ever fill the hundreds of pens and cages built so precisely to divine specification. Now she wondered how there could ever possibly be enough.

Bystanders, so recently ridiculing, stood mute with wonder. Their intellectuals and scholars had said the Creator would never tamper with the laws of nature, yet here padded the mountain lion peacefully behind two woolly lambs. Was it possible that God might, after all, open the sunny sky and pour down water? There was still time. The boat's door yet yawned a welcome.

The stream of animals seemed endless. Hour after hour they filed into the ark until the ramp was splintered with wear and soiled with droppings. Noah and his sons guided them into cages and slid catches on doors until the vessel was one great cacophony of animal noise. When finally two rabbits hopped over the doorstep, the long line that had streamed from forest and plain ended.

The last thin fingers of sunlight lay golden across the fields as Noah spoke from the ramp, his family gathered about him, their labors stilled at last. "Friends, you have seen the power of God at work today. You no longer need to take my word. You have watched the beasts enter the boat as though led by an unseen hand. God has provided for their survival upon the earth, and He longs to do the same for you. Come. Come in and be saved."

Navit, scanning the listening faces, saw fear and a new respect for Noah's message. She observed a few edging toward the ramp.

Then someone laughed. And the laughter rippled over the crowd, growing and swelling into a wild roar of released tension. The fear melted and trickled away. Somehow the parade of animals had become another joke, all in an instant. Navit felt her husband's anguish as he shouted over the laughter, fighting to bring them back to sanity.

Some pranced up the ramp two by two, mimicking the animals, only to scamper down again, creating new mirth. Others strolled home in the pleasant light of evening, secure in the pattern of sunset, sunrise. Little children asked why bears had come, all of their own accord, to Noah's boat, only to be shushed by parents who preferred not to think of the day's events. Worshipers lit fires before the images, and the rising flames flickered over gold and glittering gems while the men and women danced and sang in the flower-fragrant night.

Suddenly the bowl of Noah's meadow blazed with a light that eclipsed the foolish flames. The dancers fell into the cool grass and trembled as a radiance hovered over the mighty door of the boat.[13] Many had speculated, with cruel humor, as to how Noah would seal himself within, for the door was obviously beyond human strength to close. Now, through flashes of blinding light, they saw it swing slowly on its hinges, until, with a loud thud, it fell into place.[13]

For the second time that day, fear swept over the watcher. This time the door offered no second chance. The voice of Noah shouted no tattered invitation. The fields were still, and their very stillness screamed a warning.

* * * * *

For the hundredth time Navit fought back a tide of terror threatening to engulf her. Six days had passed in which they had done little except care for animals. At first there had barely been time to eat, but eventually they'd established a routine in which each had his assigned work; now there was a bit of time for rest and leisure. It was seventh day, sweet gift of worship and communion with God, and she tried to capture that holy

Sabbath peace that was always a renewing for her, but it eluded her. The walls of the boat closed in upon her, fierce yellow eyes of wild beasts frightened her, and the constant noise of restless animals assaulted her ears. It was nothing as she'd imagined. It had been so spare and clean when they'd filled the bins, the fragrance of dried clover mingling with the pungent aroma of wood. But now the air was close and fetid. The eight of them no longer conversed much except when necessary, for they found themselves irritable, with a tendency to snap at each other. They walked grimly in a semitwilight, waiting. When the glory of God had eased the gigantic door closed upon them, they had knelt in awe, praising Him for such comforting evidence of His presence. Now they waited, hardly knowing day from night, for the rain to fall. Outside they could hear the taunts of those surrounding the boat. Occasionally a stick or a stone thunked against the side, startling a whole sector of beasts into chain-reaction complaint.

"Can you hack your way out, Noah?"

"The sun's mighty nice out here, Noah. Not a drop of water in sight."

"How long you plan to keep that pretty, young wife of yours locked up in there, old fool?"

"These are their last days. Poor souls. Let us harbor no anger against them." Noah beckoned his family into the room that was his and Navit's and closed the door. It provided a measure of quiet.

"Dear ones, these have been horrible days. We were not prepared." His eyes moved tenderly over his wife, his sons, and the young women who had worked so hard. "We were so busy working that we gave no thought to the realities of this experience. I wish I could tell you it will grow easier, but it will not. When the rains come and the boat is dashed about upon the waves, it will demand a courage beyond any we have yet known. But you must remember that God has promised to deliver us—that no matter how severe the suffering, we *shall* survive."

Nasya burst into tears. "I am not afraid to suffer. But my family—they are lost. I shall never see my parents again, nor my brothers."

Navit went to the girl, the fair descendant of Enoch whom Noah had chosen for Japheth, and knelt at her feet, taking her hands in her own. "My child," she soothed, "I understand your tears. But perhaps some of your family *did* stand strong for God. Perhaps they died before this terrible day and sleep safely in the earth, awaiting the glorious hour of the Promised One's second coming when He shall call His true children from their graves." [14]

The girl sobbed quietly, and Navit saw a terrible sadness in the eyes of Zoe and Malka.

Loving them and remembering their long and patient labors at her side, she addressed them all: "My daughters, yours is a high calling. God saw you as worthy young women to use in His plan to cleanse the earth. It is your sons and daughters who will repopulate the world. Through you and our sons He will try again to raise up an obedient and holy people. So dry your eyes and take heart. You are precious to us, as well as to our sons. You are chosen of God."

Noah gathered them, then, about him in prayer, and Navit marveled, as always, at the friendship between her husband and his God. If her faith ever wavered, she had only to hear him pray to realize how thin the veil between heaven and earth. Their sorrows and their fears abated. They went about their evening chores with lighter hearts, even smiling now and then at some animal's antics, and the sixth day of their waiting drew to a close.

The next morning, sunlight tumbled down across the three stories of the boat, catching bits of chaff and dust in its beams. The open central area was always the lightest, and once they had finished their duties, the eight gravitated to that spot. The chants of scoffers outside mingled with the snuffling, eating sounds of the animals.

Zoe served a bowl of apricots, a tray of millet bread, and cups of warm milk. When they had finished eating, Noah smiled at his wife, adoration softening the careworn lines of his face. "Sing us a song, love. There has been little time for music, and my ears are hungry for your voice."

Shem handed her Nathan's harp, which Ona had carried all the miles through the dark forests, and Navit ran her fingers over the strings, thinking of the grandfather she'd never known. She'd lost them all for God. Her Havilah ancestors, her parents, Ona, Rimona, Nathan, Methuselah. Out of her sadness she began to sing the old song of Eve's sorrow and loss, the sweet crying of the harp clinging to her clear, melodic voice as sunlight fell rich and soft about her.

Suddenly darkness snatched the light, and a torrent of water cascaded over the window high above them. The scoffing of the crowd outside turned to wails of terror and pleadings at the huge vessel's door. The steady drumming of the rain mingled with shrieking winds, while beasts screamed and tore at restraining bars.

Noah wept for the lost, and through it all the harp and the voice of his beloved wove like a silver thread—

"Gone are the lilies of Eden,
Gone are the egrets fair;
Gone is our Friend of the evening
Who walked in the twilight there.
Gone are the innocent pleasures
That gladdened the shining days.
But ever my sin-stained heart
Rises in loving praise
To the One who speaks forgiveness,
Who lays down His life in my stead,

Who sheds the blood of His dying
Over my sinner's head . . ."

"As it was in the days of Noah, so it will be at the coming of the Son of Man. For in the days before the flood, people were eating and drinking, marrying and giving in marriage, up to the day Noah entered the ark; and they knew nothing about what would happen until the flood came and took them all away. That is how it will be at the coming of the Son of Man" (Matthew 24:37-39).

"First of all, you must understand that in the last days scoffers will come, scoffing and following their own evil desires. They will say, 'Where is this "coming" he promised? Ever since our fathers died everything goes on as it has since the beginning of creation.' But they deliberately forget that long ago by God's word the heavens existed and the earth was formed out of water and by water. By these waters also the world of that time was deluged and destroyed. By the same word the present heavens and earth are reserved for fire, being kept for the day of judgment and destruction of ungodly men. But do not forget this one thing, dear friends: With the Lord a day is like a thousand years, and a thousand years are like a day. The Lord is not slow in keeping his promise, as some understand slowness. He is patient with you, not wanting anyone to perish, but everyone to come to repentance. But the day of the Lord will come like a thief. The heavens will disappear with a roar; the elements will be destroyed by fire, and the earth and everything in it will be laid bare. Since everything will be destroyed in this way, what kind of people ought you to be? You ought to live holy and godly lives as you look forward to the day of God and speed its coming" (2 Peter 3:3-12).

¹ "So God said to Noah, . . . 'Make yourself an ark of cypress wood; make rooms in it and coat it with pitch inside and out' " (Genesis 6:13, 14).

² "By faith Noah, when warned about things not yet seen, in holy fear built an ark to save his family. By his faith he condemned the world and became heir of the righteousness that comes by faith" (Hebrews 11:7).

"[God] did not spare the ancient world when he brought the flood on its ungodly people, but protected Noah, a preacher of righteousness, and seven others" (2 Peter 2:5).

³ "For all have sinned and fall short of the glory of God" (Romans 3:23).

⁴ "But Noah found favor in the eyes of the Lord" (Genesis 6:8).

⁵ "I am going to bring floodwaters on the earth to destroy all life under the heavens, every creature that has the breath of life in it. Everything on earth will perish. But I will establish my covenant with you, and you will enter the ark—you and your sons and your wife and your sons' wives with you" (Genesis 6:17, 18).

⁶ "No shrub of the field had yet appeared on the earth and no plant of the field had yet sprung up, for the Lord God had not sent rain on the earth and there was no man to work the ground, but streams came up from the earth and watered the whole surface of the ground" (Genesis 2:5, 6).

⁷ "So God said to Noah, 'I am going to put an end to all people, for the earth is filled with violence because of them. I am surely going to destroy both them and the earth. So make yourself an ark of cypress wood; make rooms in it and coat it with pitch inside and out. This is how you are to build it: The ark is to be 450 feet long, 75 feet wide and 45 feet high. Make a roof for it and finish the ark to within 18 inches of the top. Put a door in the side of the ark and make lower, middle and upper decks. I am going to bring floodwaters on the earth to destroy all life under the heavens, every creature that has the breath of life in it. Everything on earth will perish. But I will establish my covenant with you, and you will enter the ark— you and your sons and your wife and your sons' wives with you. You are to bring into the ark two of all living creatures, male and female, to keep them alive with you. Two of every kind of bird, of every kind of animal and of every kind of

creature that moves along the ground will come to you to be kept alive. You are to take every kind of food that is to be eaten and store it away as food for you and for them' " (Genesis 6:13-21).

[8] "The LORD saw how great man's wickedness on the earth had become, and that every inclination of the thoughts of his heart was only evil all the time. The LORD was grieved that he had made man on the earth, and his heart was filled with pain. So the LORD said, 'I will wipe mankind, whom I have created, from the face of the earth—men and animals, and creatures that move along the ground, and birds of the air—for I am grieved that I have made them' " (Genesis 6:5-7).

[9] "But I will establish my covenant with you and you will enter the ark—you and your sons and your wife and your sons' wives with you" (Genesis 6:18).

[10] "After Noah was 500 years old, he became the father of Shem, Ham and Japheth" (Genesis 5:32).

[11] "You are to take every kind of food that is to be eaten and store it away as food for you and for them" (Genesis 6:21).

[12] " 'Take with you seven of every kind of clean animal, a male and its mate, and two of every kind of unclean animal, a male and its mate, and also seven of every kind of bird, male and female, to keep their various kinds alive throughout the earth.' . . . Pairs of clean and unclean animals, of birds and of all creatures that move along the ground, male and female, came to Noah and entered the ark, as God had commanded Noah" (Genesis 7:2-9).

[13] "The animals going in were male and female of every living thing, as God had commanded Noah. Then the Lord shut him in" (Genesis 7:16).

[14] "Listen, I tell you a mystery. We will not all sleep, but we will all be changed—in a flash, in the twinkling of an eye, at the last trumpet. For the trumpet will sound, the dead will be raised imperishable, and we will be changed" (1 Corinthians 15:51, 52).

Find a "Valley of Peace" in today's ═══world.═══

Find out more about living at peace with God. Write us and we will mail you information on any of these topics.

- ☐ Knowing Christ—the Promised One—and how He relieves guilt
- ☐ His soon return to this earth
- ☐ Why Seventh-day Adventists worship on Saturday
- ☐ Creation of the world
- ☐ What happens when a person dies
- ☐ Prophecies made in the Bible
- ☐ What Adventists believe

I would like:
- ☐ To study the Bible on my own. Please enroll me in a Bible correspondence course.
- ☐ Someone to study the Bible with me.
- ☐ Someone to pray for me.
- ☐ A personal visit from a Christian in my area.
- ☐ The address of the nearest Seventh-day Adventist church.
- ☐ Other (specify): _____

_____

Mail to: Adventist Information Ministry
Andrews University, Berrien Springs, Michigan 49104

Date _____

Name _____

Address _____

City _____ For faster service

State/Prov _____ call toll-free at

Zip/PC _____ **1-800-253-3000**

Phone _____ (in Alaska, **1-800-253-3002**).